Guaranteed Justice

M A Comley

D1534027

OTHER BOOKS BY
NEW YORK TIMES BEST SELLING AUTHOR
M. A. COMLEY

Cruel Justice

Impeding Justice

Final Justice

Foul Justice

Guaranteed Justice

Ultimate Justice

Virtual Justice

Hostile Justice

Tortured Justice

Rough Justice (coming Jan 2015)

Blind Justice (A Justice novella)

Evil In Disguise (Based on true events)

Forever Watching You (#1 D I Miranda Carr Thrillers)

Torn Apart (Hero Series #1)

End Result (Hero Series #2)

Sole Intention (Intention Series #1)

Grave Intention (Intention Series #2)

It's A Dog's Life (A Lorne Simpkins short story)

ACKNOWLEDGMENTS

As always love and best wishes to my wonderful Mum for the role she plays in my career. Special thanks to my superb editor Stefanie, and my wonderful cover artist Karri. Thanks also to Joseph my amazing proof reader.

For Sammy, you will live on forever in my heart.

Licence Notes.

GUARANTEED JUSTICE

PROLOGUE

Linda Carter glanced the handsome onlooker's way for what must have been the hundredth time. His broad smile beamed back at her.

Abigail's elbow connected with her ribs. She winced.

"Girl, does he have the hots for you or what?"

"Behave yourself, Abigail." Linda blushed. She hoped he wouldn't notice in the dimmed lights of the nightclub.

After another dig in the ribs, she issued her friend a warning glare.

"Oh my God! He's coming this way," Abigail said behind her hand.

Before Linda had the chance to look in his direction, she felt his arm slink around her waist and his hot breath heating up her neck.

"Oh my God" is right!

Abigail drifted away through the crowd. Linda and the hunk danced for the next half an hour or so before they moved over to the bar. He bought the drinks while Linda went to the ladies' to powder her nose.

She returned and downed her drink in one gulp before he eagerly steered her back onto the dance floor. Was it a coincidence that the music tempo changed to a slow number? He held her tightly and rubbed his groin against hers. A tingly sensation took over her body as his kisses burned first her earlobe then her cheek.

His hot breath lingered by her ear, and he whispered, "What do you say we get outta here?"

Linda didn't need asking twice. He was easily the best-looking guy in the club, and he wanted to leave with her. What more could a girl want? She nervously moistened her lips, then nodded her agreement.

He took her by the hand and led her through the heaving club and the main door. She smiled shyly as he shared a private joke with the doorman.

"Where are we going?" Linda asked sheepishly after they reached his Ferrari.

"Thought we'd go back to my place for a nightcap. Is that all right with you?"

She answered him by jumping in the passenger seat. They engaged in light, flirty conversation for the next ten minutes or so before he guided the car into an underground car park. He applied the handbrake, then slid a lazy hand up her thigh. He lingered at the hem of her mini-skirt for a second or two.

Her eyes automatically clenched shut, and she held her breath, anticipating his next movement.

He surprised her by laughing softly and ran his tongue up her right cheek. Linda shuddered as the excitement stirred.

"Not here. Come on," he told her, his tone sexy and full of promise.

Linda stumbled from the car as if drunk with happiness when he held the door open for her.

"Oops! Steady girl," she reprimanded herself, pulling her shoulders back. She giggled and asked, words slurred, "You wicked man. Did you slip an extra voddy in my drink?"

His hand covered his chest, and he innocently fluttered his eyelashes at her. "Moi?"

Then he gripped her elbow, and they moved toward the elevator in the corner. The bell tinged, and the doors slid open. With every passing floor, his kisses became hotter and more urgent, until finally, with Linda gasping for air, the doors opened to an illuminated view of London.

"Wow! You live in a penthouse." She made her way over to the full-length window, her feet sinking into the luxury carpet beneath.

He stood behind her and wrapped his arms around her waist. "Sod the view. I have something crying out for your attention." His tone was flat.

She felt a stiffness rubbing up and down her backside. She didn't have to be a genius to figure out what it was.

In a flash he'd turned her to face him. His arms pulled hers behind her. His handsome face had contorted with what appeared to be anger.

Confusion made her ask, "Is something wrong?" Her head swam. Was that the drink or the confusion?

Then she heard a click behind her back and thought she felt cold metal clasp her wrists.

His lips turned up at the corner. "You've been begging for this for weeks. Now you're going to get it."

Scared, Linda wriggled her arms, trying to release her hands. It dawned on her that they were being restrained by cuffs. "Please, I don't know what you mean."

"You know exactly what I mean. Your type take pleasure in leading men on. You prick teaser. Well, I'll teach you. Take your punishment, or I'll go after your sister, bitch..."

Linda opened her mouth, but before she got the chance to scream, his mouth roughly claimed hers. His hands tore at the buttons on her silk blouse. Linda squirmed, but his superior strength overpowered her feeble effort.

It wasn't long before the metallic taste of blood ran between her teeth and down the back of her throat.

His hand thrust up her skirt, and he tore her panties aside. She sucked in a panicked breath.

Everything went black.

* * *

When Linda Carter regained consciousness, she felt dirty. Disgusted. More so with herself than with the bastard who had raped her.

She was lying in an alley. It took her a while to get her bearings and recognise her surroundings. She heard the drunken revellers leaving the nightclub. Even saw a few of the men relieving themselves against the alley walls before they staggered back out onto the high street.

All of them were oblivious to the fact that Linda was in desperate need of medical care.

Please. Somebody please help me!

The attack was a fuzzy image in her mind. When she ran a cautious hand over her limbs, she flinched at the pain her body was in. Her clothes were torn, and her knickers had been removed.

How could she have put herself in such a dangerous position? One minute she was dancing and enjoying herself on the dance floor with her friend; the next she was being led outside by the charmer who had been eyeing her up all evening. Foolishly and against her better judgement, she had allowed him to entice her to leave the safety of the club.

Why did I go with him? When he started to lead her out of the club her inner voice had warned her to be careful, but blinded by his handsome features and charming nature, she had obstinately refused to listen.

Her legs wobbled beneath her as she tried her hardest to get off the cold, damp ground.

Finally she found the strength, with the aid of the knobbly wall behind her, to successfully hoist herself to her feet. The pain forced her to steady herself for a moment. Once she'd caught her breath she hobbled, inching her way slowly up the length of the alley towards the entrance.

Every time she put her left foot on the ground, the pain from her injured ankle surged up her leg and rattled through her aching body. She winced as she battled through the discomfort.

When she finally reached the opening onto the high street, she raised her hand to hail an approaching taxi. She felt relieved when he pulled to a stop in front of her instead of the drunken group messing around about fifty feet ahead, though the screech of tyres in the dimly lit street jangled her frayed nerves.

"Where to, love?" the driver asked. His eyebrows knitted together as he studied her in his rear-view mirror. When she didn't answer, he turned in his seat. He inhaled in a startled breath and mumbled, "Jesus... I'm taking you to the hospital, right away." That was the night Linda Carter's life changed forever.

CHAPTER ONE

"My God! Is she all right?" Fiona sank into the worn leather sofa as she listened to the ward sister on the phone, giving news about Fiona's sister Linda.

Her Chinese flatmate, Ami—who had also been woken by the telephone ringing at two in the morning—sat down beside her. She tugged Fiona's arm. "What is it? Has something happened to Linda?"

Both women wore their towelling robes, still half asleep.

"Shhh... Wait a minute... Sorry. Please go on." She felt the colour drain from her cheeks, and her mind raced as she chewed over the information the nurse was giving her. She grabbed Ami's hand and nestled it in her lap.

Ami rested her cheek on her shoulder, and Fiona heard her let out a long sigh.

Words caught in Fiona's throat. "May I come in and see her?"

"Maybe in the morning. We've just given her a sedative to help calm her down. Her ankle is broken, so she'll need to go for surgery tomorrow afternoon," the ward sister replied.

"I understand. I'll have to clear it with my boss, but I'll try to get there first thing. If she's still awake, tell her I love her and that I'm thinking of her."

"Of course. Try to get some sleep and try not to worry too much. Your sister is safe with us, now."

Fiona hung up and sobbed uncontrollably—something she hadn't done in years—for a full five minutes. Ami cried also and held Fiona's shuddering body tightly in a vice-like grip.

Eventually, Fiona opened up and repeated the information the ward sister had shared. "Oh, Ami. If I had gone with her tonight, this would never have happened. If I hadn't been so involved with my blasted paperwork..."

"You can't punish yourself like this. Sometimes things happen that are out of our control. Besides, Linda was supposed to be with her friends, wasn't she?" Ami consoled her quietly.

"You're right, of course. I'm not sure what the ins and outs are of what happened, yet. Why or how did she get separated from her friends? It's so out of character for Linda to go off with someone she met in a club. She's always been the sensible one. Whatever possessed her to do such a thing?"

Ami shrugged and stood up. "I'll get us a mug of hot milk. It'll help us sleep. Linda will need us to be strong for her. She'll get through this. We'll make sure she does." She left the room.

Fresh tears ran down Fiona's cheeks as her sister's beautiful face flooded her mind. Please let there be no permanent damage, either physically or mentally. During their childhood, Linda had always been the one to whom the boys had flocked. It hadn't been surprising when she'd been labelled the most beautiful girl at school. She had endured copious amounts of jealousy from the other girls who'd been cast aside by the boys clambering to make a date with Linda. Fiona had found it all amusing, the way the boys queued up to talk to Linda in the school playground throughout their school years.

Not once had she ever been envious of her sister's popularity or good looks. It was unthinkable that her sister's popularity would have led to something as harrowing as the night's events.

Ami came back with two mugs of warm milk and handed one to Fiona. "She'll be fine. We'll make sure of that, hon."

Shaking her head slowly, Fiona said, "I'm not so sure. She has a fragile spirit. You don't know her like I do." Ami's head dropped onto her chest, and Fiona could have kicked herself for saying something unintentionally unkind. "Sorry. I didn't mean anything by that. Me and my big mouth."

Ami raised her angelic Chinese face, and blinked her intense black eyes a few times. "I know you didn't mean anything by that. Since I moved in, you two have been like sisters to me. I've only known you for just over a year, but you both mean the world to me."

"I'm sorry, Ami. Just ignore me. Linda and I both feel the same way about you, too. Come on, let's try to get some sleep. You've got college tomorrow, and I've got to inch my way into my boss's good books."

They each went to their respective bedrooms, but sleep evaded Fiona for the rest of the night. Every time her eyes fluttered shut, all she could imagine was Linda being attacked and mauled by a faceless brute of a man.

Fiona's teeth ground together as she thought up ways to exact her revenge, most of which involved using a sharp implement. She shuddered the images away. She knew she could never hurt another human being like that.

The next morning, Fiona rose at seven and jumped in the shower, during which she figured out the telephone conversation she intended to have with her boss at nine to wangle the day off. She had to come up with some plausible excuse. He wasn't the type to be satisfied with a naff excuse like 'I've got a stinking cold' or 'I overslept because the alarm didn't go off.' She couldn't possibly tell him the truth.

When nine o'clock arrived, she swallowed hard and dialled the private line to his office. "Rick? It's Fiona. I hate to dump this on you first thing, and I know we have an important meeting with corporate clients today, but I need to take the day off." She closed her eyes, anticipating the barrage of words that would come her way.

"Fiona, I know you well enough by now to know that it must be extremely important for you to take time off on such a significant day. Do what you have to do, and come back soon."

Wow. His reaction floored her. Maybe Rick had picked up on something in her tone.

Whatever the reason behind his sudden understanding nature, she was extremely grateful. "Hope everything goes well with the Tyler account. I'll definitely be in tomorrow."

"It will. You've done all the groundwork, anyway. All I have to do is get them to sign the contract. Take as much time as you need, girl."

"Thanks, Rick. It's appreciated. Good luck."

"You too," he replied, and they both hung up.

"Well, that went better than planned," Fiona said when Ami walked into the room still wearing her night shirt and carrying a bowl of cornflakes.

"Just the hospital to deal with, now. Are you sure you don't want me to come with you? I have a free lesson, first thing."

Fiona screwed up her nose and shook her head. "I'm heading off now. I'd rather have a few minutes alone with Linda, if you don't mind. You know, assess her state of mind."

"The offer still stands, but I absolutely understand."

Fiona picked up her Yves Saint Laurent Muse designer handbag, and her coat from the coat rack, and headed for the front door. "See you later."

Chewing on a mouthful of cornflakes, Ami nodded.

The traffic around London was horrendous as usual, but Fiona stopped caring about the length of time the trip was taking her by focussing on her sister, instead. As much as her usually organised brain warned her to remain calm for Linda's sake, it didn't stop her seething at the injustice of the situation. Linda was such a gentle soul who definitely didn't deserve to be treated like that.

Not that any woman deserved to be raped. The situation still surprised Fiona; she always considered her sister to be the cautious one, as far as men were concerned. She usually chose her boyfriends after several weeks of consideration. She was never one of those girls who jumped into bed with a guy after meeting him a few hours before.

Which was why Fiona found it hard to fathom how her sister had got herself into such a deplorable, unthinkable position.

Finally, she arrived at St Thomas' hospital. She asked at reception where she could find her sister and rushed through the corridors, her heels clicking on the tiled floor and echoing off the walls.

Thankfully, Linda had been allocated a private ward. Fiona tapped on the door lightly before pushing it open.

The sight that greeted her caused her to inhale sharply. Fiona was both sickened and repulsed by the bruises that had caused Linda's face to swell. She was almost unrecognisable. Her left eye was a mere slit; the swelling surrounding it was a rainbow of colours.

Okay, now. Remain calm. Don't break down. Fiona approached the bed and kissed her sister gently on her bandaged forehead. Then she sat on the bed beside her battered sister.

"Oh, Fi. What did I do to deserve this?" Linda asked her voice croaky and full of emotion.

Tears welled up as Fiona studied her sister's appalling injuries. She swallowed down the lump in her throat and patted Linda's hand. "You mustn't blame yourself, sweetheart. You don't or can't have any control over another person's instincts. If this man set out to hurt a stranger, you were just unfortunate, to be in the wrong place at the wrong time."

Linda remained silent for a few seconds, but as fresh tears cascaded down her puffy cheeks, she whispered, "He wasn't a stranger..."

CHAPTER TWO

Lorne clutched at the excruciating pain attacking her sides as tears streamed down her face.

Tony glanced up at her and shook his head. "Some bloody support you are."

His hand sunk into the mud behind him as he tried to retrieve his false leg. Annoyance creased up his eyes. He held out his other arm in her direction. "When you've quite finished laughing at me, any chance you can help a disabled man out of this damn quagmire?"

Lorne knew she shouldn't laugh at him, knew he'd exact his revenge on her somehow in the not-too-distant future, but the way he'd tumbled reminded her of one of those old black and white films she used to watch as a child. In her youth, the Three Stooges had held her captivated for hours.

When she'd married Tony six months ago, she had no notion her life would be filled with so much laughter and love that had been missing throughout her previous marriage to Tom. Although, looking at the way he was sinking in the mud around their two-acre paddock, Tony wasn't doing much laughing at the moment.

She ventured forward on the outskirts of the innocent-looking mud patch and held out her hand to help. Their fingers touched tentatively. She reached further, not wishing to spoil the new pink wellies her daughter, Charlie, had bought her the previous weekend. Her hand slipped into his.

Instead of Lorne pulling Tony out of the mud, he jerked his hand quickly and pulled her on top of him. "Laugh at me at your peril, Lorne Warner."

Her screams of disbelief quickly extinguished, replaced by hoots of laughter. "You really don't like me missing out on anything, do you?" she asked as he placed a muddy hand either side of her face and looked at her, his eyes brimming with love.

"For better, for worse, the vicar said. It doesn't get much worse than this."

They laughed before he kissed her deeply.

The truth was that the mess they were sitting in at the moment was a breeze, compared to what they'd both encountered through life thus far. As an ex-MI6 agent, Tony had been tortured several times for the sake of queen and country. His final mission, after he'd been captured and publicly tortured by the Taliban, had been the one where he'd actually lost his leg. So far, Lorne had been utterly impressed by the way he'd adapted and coped with his disability.

Lorne's own life experiences had hardly been run-of-the-mill, either. In the line of duty as one of the Met's best serving detective inspectors, she'd met her fair share of callous villains and come close to losing more than a limb several times herself, in the last decade, mostly at the hands of her archenemy the Unicorn.

The Unicorn had succeeded in killing her partner in the force and had kidnapped and raped her daughter. Those two events had done more damage to her mentally than anything he could've conjured up physically, if ever he'd had the chance. There had been an incident where she had found herself naked in his presence, but Lorne, being Lorne, had managed to squirm her way out of the situation before the Unicorn had laid his mucky paws on her.

Their kiss ended, and Lorne let out a satisfied sigh.

"What was that for?" Tony asked.

"Just thinking."

"About?"

"How we got to be here. The obstacles we've both had to overcome. You more than me."

"Come on. Help me up."

Lorne salvaged Tony's prosthetic limb before they attempted to leave the mud. They grunted and groaned as they fought against the stickiness and slipperiness of the mud, then laughed at the way it made slurping noises as they trudged through it back to the safety of the grassy part of the paddock.

He took her in his arms and smiled down at her. "If we hadn't been together, I doubt I would have got through the last six months, darling."

Lorne shook her head and wrinkled her nose. "I doubt that's true, Tony. You're one of life's survivors. You wouldn't know what failure was if it was tattooed on your forehead and you had to look at it in the mirror every morning."

"Have I told you lately how much I love you?" he asked, running a muddy finger down the length of her nose.

She pretended to think about her reply. "Umm...not since this morning. Let's grab a coffee and see if the post has come yet."

Tony strapped his artificial leg in place and slipped an arm around her shoulder as they set off for the main house.

"Are you sure you want to set out on this new venture? Isn't it a bit soon?" he asked tentatively.

Lorne glanced up at him as they continued walking. "I need to do it. I love having this place. Love the fact that we're able to save and nurture all these animals that are crying out to be cared for, but there is still something missing. I thought we'd been through all this before I'd applied for the diploma."

"I know we did. But I kind of like having you around twenty-four, seven." He gave her shoulder a squeeze.

That was when her brain really kicked in and she felt the beginning of a plan hatching. "I don't know why I didn't think of it before. How dumb of me. We could both run the agency. Both be PIs..."

He stopped abruptly and turned to face her. "Now, wait just a minute." His arm swept around him. "Have you forgotten about this place? Who's going to run it?"

Lorne waved her hand in front of her, pooh-poohing his question as if the answer were obvious. "Don't worry about that. I have someone special in mind to look after this place. Hey, we'll still be around to do the majority of the chores. Neither of us would be able to cope with sitting on our backsides not doing anything all day. We need stimulation. Need our brains to be functioning properly."

He tutted and shook his head. "Once you have a plan in place, there really is no stopping you, is there?"

"Nope. What do you say?"

"I say, we talk about this over a mug of coffee before I start cleaning out the kennels."

They were both chuckling about the antics of Henry, their Border collie, chasing the chickens in the yard outside, when they stepped into the kitchen of the farmhouse they'd purchased four months earlier.

The property had been bought on the cheap because the former owners had been in financial difficulties and unable to pay the exorbitant mortgage after the economy had crashed. Lorne and Tony had a couple of flats for sale that they'd renovated, and offered one of the flats in exchange for a reduction on the farmhouse, which was set in ten acres of land. The vendor had virtually snapped their hands off. The transaction had been good for everyone concerned.

The farmhouse, which was in need of minor renovations, came with a kennel block, a two-acre paddock, a small wooded area—ideal to keep their wood-burning stove running during the winter months—and several barns, that could be turned into holiday lets, if needed. Off the main house was an adjoining two-bedroomed annex that had Lorne's father's name written all over it.

After they moved in, Lorne had asked the builders who'd carried out the renovations on the flats she had updated, if they would knock the annex into shape for her father to live in, as a complete surprise to Sam Collins.

A month after Tony and Lorne had moved in, her father had visited the farmhouse. That was when Lorne had dangled the idea in front of him. Her father had gone home that evening and immediately contacted an estate agent. The agent had told him that if he wanted a quick sale on his property, he would need to sell it at a lower price than he was expecting to get after owning the house for over twenty years. Lorne had reassured him it was the right thing to do and that the money side of things didn't really matter.

He sold the house after a couple of weeks, and by the time the sale had gone through, the builders had finished his 'little house' as he called it. He'd moved in before the paint had time to dry.

Since the move, her father had seemed like his old self, walking around as if he had a purpose in life. He'd been drifting like a lost soul since Lorne's mother had died of breast cancer four years earlier, struggling daily to cope with his retirement from the force and being thrust into living a solitary life. He'd been crying out for more of a social life with his two daughters and their respective partners just to keep his sanity intact.

Her father greeted them at the back door, his face beaming as he studied the state of their clothes. "What on earth have you two been up to?"

"Tony was sampling the mud out by the paddock to see if it would be viable to sell it to the health spa up the road," Lorne told him as she walked over to the kitchen sink to wash the mud off her face.

Her father laughed. "I'm not sure I believe you on that score, dear."

Lorne dried her face and hands, pecked her father on the cheek and headed into the hallway. "I'm just going to get out of these clothes, then I have a proposition for you, Dad."

She could hear her father asking Tony what she meant, but she disappeared up the stairs before she heard her husband's response.

Lorne ignored the pink large-flowered vinyl wallpaper adorning the walls of her boudoir and went over to the wardrobe in the corner. As she pulled on her clean clothes, she mulled over how much better the room would look after she was done with it. She couldn't wait to put her designer skills into action; she had big ideas for the master bedroom. She'd already made up a mood board for the room. The board contained several magazine clippings of furniture she had her eye on, swatches of material she had chosen for the bedding and curtains, and even a sample of the carpet she had earmarked for the room.

But the changes would have to wait until more funds became available. At present, all their money had been set aside for feeding the menagerie of animals they had already rescued in their short time at the property. It hadn't taken long for word to spread that Lorne and Tony never turned away an animal in need. Which meant that at the moment, they shared their home with ten dogs, five cats, and a flock of geese that had narrowly escaped being made into foie gras thanks to Lorne's timely intervention.

Several old sheep grazed in the field next to her father's annex, and the newest member of their animal family was a donkey that was due to arrive that morning. That was why Lorne and Tony had been out by the paddock earlier, where they had accidentally ended up frolicking in the mud. The object of the exercise had been to ensure that the paddock was safe for the little fellow before putting him in his new home. The poor mite had spent his entire young life living in a grubby barn, up to his knees in his own faeces, without a fresh blade of grass ever having passed his lips.

When Lorne had heard of the poor creature's plight, it had taken all her strength not to punch the owner on the nose. The second he'd shown her the donkey's living conditions, Lorne's heart immediately went out to the poor animal. She had paid the man two hundred pounds, and not yet having access to a horsebox, she had asked him if he would deliver Hercules to the house. The vile owner had ummed and ahhed before he reluctantly agreed.

She arrived back in the kitchen just as the post shot through the letterbox. Lorne skipped up the hallway and pounced on the mixture of brown and white envelopes. Placing the brown bills to the back of the pile, she tore open the A5-sized envelope she'd been expecting and whooped for joy. Punching a fist in the air she let out a relieved, "Yes!"

There was no licence in the UK at present for private investigators, but having a diploma from one of the leading PI courses went a long way to setting up a PI firm. Lorne laughed to herself as she wandered back to the kitchen. *Maybe I'll be the female version of Mike Hammer.*

"I see you got it, then," Tony said, shaking his head with amusement.

"Got what?" Lorne's father asked, confused.

She handed him the laminated certificate and waited for his reaction. She laughed when his eyes almost popped out of his ageing face.

"A PI! Are you insane?"

That was not how she had anticipated her father would react to the news. "Why not?"

Her father poured the boiling water into the mugs, stirred the coffees, and set the mugs on the kitchen table as the three of them pulled out their chairs and sat down, some of them more heavily than others.

Sam Collins let out a deep breath. His gaze met hers. "For heaven's sake, Lorne. What about this place? All this was to be your new exciting venture, or have you forgotten that?"

Lorne looked over at Tony for help, but he shrugged once and looked down at his mug of coffee. She was on her own, on this one. "Okay, Dad. You're right; of course you are. But…"

She paused for a second or two as she searched for the right words, all the while becoming more nervous under her father's intense stare. She twisted her mug on the table in front of her before taking a sip of the scalding hot liquid. Great. Now she'd have a blister on the roof of her mouth to have to contend with for the rest of the day, too.

She cleared her throat and looked her father in the eye as she'd always done when her determined streak came to the fore. "Dad, you know me—"

"Huh, I should. You're my flesh and blood, after all. But I sometimes wonder if I really know you at all, Lorne. Over the years, you've had some hare-brained schemes, but this...this definitely tops the lot."

Lorne frowned. "Why? I'm not sure what it is you're so against, Dad." It was difficult for her to push down the feeling of hurt from his reaction.

Instead of answering her, her father turned to Tony. "And you're all right with this?"

Officially stuck in the middle, Tony rose to his feet. "I think it best if I leave you two alone to discuss this. I'll be in the lounge. Give me a shout when you're done."

Gobsmacked, Lorne's jaw dropped open as her eyes bore into his traitorous retreating back. That day was turning out to be full of surprises. Both the men in her life had reacted to the situation by giving her the cold shoulder, something she was neither used to nor appreciated.

"I take it Tony agrees with me?" her father asked, a note of triumph in his voice.

Lorne turned back to her father and gathered his hand in hers. "Why all the anger, Dad?"

He seemed shocked by her question. "Oh darling, it's not anger. It's concern. In the past three years, you've changed your mind so many times I can hardly keep up with you. This was to be your and Tony's new start. Now you want to start putting your life at risk again. What about the animals? What's going to happen to them?"

"The animals will be well-cared for."

"By whom?" he asked through slanted eyes.

"Umm...Well, I thought you could help out there."

Her father shook his head, and the creases in his forehead disappeared. He smiled and tilted his head. "Oh, you did, did you? You do realise that I'm not getting any younger."

"I know, Dad, but..."

Amused, he laughed when he understood what she was getting at. "I need to earn my keep, is that it?"

She squeezed his hand affectionately and felt relieved that his anger or concern had momentarily dissipated. "Would you like to hear my plan? My revised plan for this place."

"I'm all ears."

"Okay, here goes. No interrupting. Just hear me out. Promise?"

Her father slid his hand from under hers and leaned back in his chair, his arms folded tightly across his chest.

She inhaled deeply. "First off, I need to get out there and help people. I can't keep going back to the force, though, Dad. You know I don't fit into their male dominated society. So I figured becoming a PI would be the next best thing. I love helping the animals out, and I would never want to give up this place. However, I have a niggling doubt that something is missing. I don't feel complete."

She leaned over the table and whispered, "I'm doing this as much for Tony as for me. Do you seriously think he's going to be happy mucking out kennels for the rest of his life? He's getting used to his leg now, and once that happens, he'll need more stimulation than picking up dog turds all day long. I know he doesn't seem keen on the idea now, but I'm sure once the cases start rolling in, he'll be the first one sifting through them, pouncing on the juicier ones." She sat back in her chair and laughed.

"Can I talk now?"

She smiled and nodded.

"I can understand where you're coming from, especially where Tony is concerned, but I just don't think you've thought everything through thoroughly. Like I say, I'm not getting any younger. It takes two of you to run this place as it is now, and you're expecting me to do it on my own." He raised a hand to silence Lorne before she could speak. "You've had your say, without interruptions. Please give me the same courtesy."

She squeezed her lips together and ran two fingers over them, pretending to zip her mouth shut.

Her father rolled his eyes. "All this PI stuff can be tough, you know. Have you considered how you're going to do background checks on people, et cetera? There are certain things you won't be able to find out on the Internet. Obviously, it depends what type of cases come in. All the same, I don't think you've done enough homework on the subject. Although I do understand your need to want to help people, nothing gave me greater pleasure than to help you in your investigation when Charlie was kidnapped. However, I was helping an active police investigation. We had certain files and other outside agencies we could call on for help. That's how you and Tony met, if you remember?"

"I'm hardly likely to forget how we met, Dad. Oops, sorry. Can I speak?"

Her father smirked and nodded, then took a sip of coffee.

"I didn't go into this project without some thought, Dad. I'm still in touch with DCI Roberts—who is constantly begging me to return, I hasten to add. He's aware of my intentions and has offered to lend a hand when he can. He understands me, knows that I wouldn't abuse any help offered. I know there'll be certain things he can't help me with, wearing his jobsworth hat, but that's where I'm hoping Katy will be willing to step in."

"Katy?"

"My former partner. Once I tell her what I'm up to, I hope she'll volunteer to assist and carry out certain activities for me that Roberts won't be able to give the go-ahead for."

"That sounds mighty dangerous for Katy, Lorne. She could lose her job for helping you out, if she gets caught."

Lorne gulped down some more of her coffee. "I know. Anyway, if they kick her out, she can always come work for me."

"You're assuming that the business will be a success, then."

"Of course." Lorne picked up the diploma she'd gained through the night classes she'd attended without her father knowing of it. "This diploma is linked to a website of reputable PIs. I'm sure I'll get plenty of business coming my way from there. Roberts and Katy have promised to put the word around for me, too. I don't really want to go down the route of taking an ad out in the local press, but if I have to, I will. Once the jobs start streaming in, Tony will want some of the action. I'm sure we'll be able to count on his contacts at MI6 on the odd occasion to help out, too.

"You know how these things work, Dad. Between us, we're all well connected, and if it means getting criminals off the streets, then I'm sure everyone will be clambering to lend us a helping hand. We'll be saving them a job, anyway."

"And this place?"

"If you'll be kind enough to take over the everyday running of the place, Tony and I will help out when we can. The PI business will probably take a while to get going. At the weekends, when Charlie comes to visit, she'll lend a hand. She's always keen to help out with the animals. I was actually going to ask her to take over the place eventually—not now, but after she leaves school. She loves animals. What do you think?"

His mouth twisted, and he closed one eye. "I'm sure she'd jump at the chance to work here or run the place, but what about her education—her higher education, I mean?"

"I'm not going to force her into going to uni, Dad. We've discussed it a few times, and she's not bothered about going to uni and getting into debt at such a young age. She's more mature than other kids her age because of what she's been through over the past few years. I'm willing to let her make her own decisions in life."

"Ha! If I know Charlie, she'll be wanting to team up with her mum in the PI business. You remember what she said to you in her hospital bed when we got her back from the Unicorn?"

"I do indeed. She wanted to sign up for the Met there and then, the little minx. Nah, I'm sure she'll love running this place for me. Is it safe to call Tony back in now?"

Her father tutted and smiled. "I'm sure he'll be grateful he's not caught up in a crossfire any longer."

Lorne leaned back in the chair and called over her shoulder, "Tony! It's safe to return now."

They heard the news on the TV being switched off and Lorne's husband, looking kind of sheepish, rejoined them.

"So? What's been decided in my absence?" Tony asked, sitting down next to Lorne.

Her father spoke first. "Well, as my daughter has it all figured out, I'm willing to give her suggestion a go. I'll do what I can around this place on the proviso that when you're not busy PIing, you'll promise to toe the line around here. Actually, I'd like to help out on that side of things once Charlie takes over the reins here."

"Whoa, hold on a minute. What's this about Charlie?" Tony asked Lorne.

She grinned broadly and patted the top of his hand. "You leave everything to me, darling. I have it all worked out up here." Lorne tapped the side of her head with her forefinger and winked at him.

"Oh, God. That's what I was afraid of," Tony mumbled, before Lorne clipped him round the head.

CHAPTER THREE

Fiona, Linda, and Ami were sitting on the sofa in the lounge, each of them hoping that one of the others would be the first to speak.

Finally, Fiona took the initiative, her voice buoyant and far from downhearted. "I say we have Indian tonight. My treat, of course."

Ami cringed.

Fiona realised she had come across too jovial. If she could have, she would have given herself a hard kick. The three of them had been tiptoeing around each other for a good hour, and it left her feeling more than a little restless. She stood up and searched the dresser drawer for the takeaway menu, and handed it to her sister.

Linda shook her head and pushed the folded piece of paper away. "I couldn't eat a thing."

"Aww, come on, Sis. You have to keep your strength up."

"Do I?" Linda snapped back. "For what, exactly? More disbelieving questions from the police?" She buried her head in her hands and sobbed so hard her shoulders shook.

Ami took it as her cue to leave the room.

Fiona knelt on the floor in front of her distraught sister, and rocked her gently in her arms. "Shh...now. You've cried enough tears over what that bastard has done, sweetheart. The police said they'll be visiting that rapist shit, Gibson. Let's just see what they come up with, shall we?"

After pulling out of Fiona's arms, Linda took a hankie from her sleeve, dried her eyes, and blew her nose on it. "But you heard what the detective said. It'll be his word against mine."

Fiona knew that. She was still confused as to why her sister hadn't at least tried to fight off her attacker. As yet Linda hadn't gone over the events leading up to the attack, and Fiona thought it would be best to leave the questioning until her sister was better equipped emotionally to deal with the painful memory of that night, which she had so far attempted to block out. The police had questioned her before Fiona had arrived, and Linda had found the questioning so traumatic that both Ami and Fiona had skirted around what had happened with the police since.

Now that Linda had the courage to refer to her attacker, Fiona seized the opportunity to find out more. "Can you tell me what happened, sweetie?"

Linda's eyes widened as if the thought of going over the details again would completely destroy her.

Fiona rubbed the back of her sister's hand, which was now winding a fresh tissue through her fingers. "Only if you feel up to it, of course."

Sucking in a deep shuddering breath, Linda kept her gaze focused on the rug beside Fiona. "Abigail and I were on the dance floor when Gibson joined us. We started chatting, and Abigail left us to it. I was so enthralled with him that I barely noticed she had gone…"

"Go on," Fiona encouraged quietly.

Linda let out a huge sigh and tucked a stray section of hair behind her left ear. "We danced for a while and then had a couple of drinks at the bar. I didn't have many, I swear. Gibson pulled me onto the floor just as the slow numbers were starting, and that's when he asked if we could leave. The place was crowded, far busier than usual. There was some kind of hen party going on. I just wanted to get out of there."

Fiona could tell her sister was trying to shuffle her thoughts into some kind of chronological order. She waited patiently.

Linda swallowed hard. "We went outside. The bouncer and Gibson shared a secret joke. He told me that there wouldn't be a problem for us to get back into the nightclub when we wanted to return. Anyway, we went in search of his car. Things were going great until we reached his penthouse."

Fiona nodded, urging her to go on.

"All of a sudden, he pulled my arms behind me and put something around my wrists. At first I didn't know what it was, then I realised it was handcuffs. Everything happened so fast.

"I know we had this discussion years ago that if we found ourselves in such a situation, we should lash out, scratch the offender or scream out for help. But I just couldn't. His mouth was clamped over mine like a vice. I tried to bite him, but it was too difficult." Tears sprang from Linda's eyes and began running down her cheeks.

Fiona took the near-shredded tissue from her sister's grasp and dabbed the salty line away. "Come on, hon. You're doing so well."

"He covered my mouth with his and placed his hand up my skirt. Fi, I was so frightened. By then, I would have done just about anything to get out of there alive. The look in his eyes was so... I thought he was going to kill me."

"I'd be frantic too, if I'd been in your shoes. How did your ankle get busted up?"

"I'm not sure. I passed out about then. Although, I do hazily remember that he threatened me. I felt him do unspeakable things to me. I swear I wasn't drunk. Maybe he used that date rape drug or something, I don't know. My heart was pounding out of control..."

By now, Fiona's own heart was pounding like a runaway train in her chest. "What threat did he make, love?"

"He told me, if I didn't comply...that he'd come after you next."

"What?"

Linda nodded as more tears spilled from her red eyes. Fiona got up from the floor and sat on the sofa next to her sister.

"I didn't want the same thing to happen to you, Fi. I was about to give in, but I passed out. It didn't stop me feeling his grubby hands on me, though."

Fiona covered her face with her hands then ran them through her hair. "Oh, Linda. If only you could've struck out at him. We could've—would've—dealt with the consequences after you were out of harm's way. You're always putting others first, when you should be thinking of your own needs."

"I'm not so sure. How can you take the word of a rapist? I wasn't aware that Gibson even knew you."

"That's what I wanted to ask you, Linda. How do you know this lowlife?"

Linda turned to face her. "He's always at the club. A friend of a friend, you might say. He used to have a girlfriend up until a few weeks ago. He's been eyeing me up for weeks, and I suppose he finally plucked up enough courage to talk to me this week. I wish he hadn't bothered. What's going to happen now? The police said they're going to see him, to ask his side of the story, but you can imagine what the little shit will be telling them, can't you?"

"The police will find out the truth, love. He may be a slimy git, but they'll pick up if he's telling the truth or not. And as for him coming after me, we'll see about that. If I get my hands on him, I'll rip his balls off and feed them to him, one after the other."

Linda smiled and pecked her on the cheek. "For your sake and his, I hope the two of you never meet."

Fiona privately hoped she would have the pleasure of meeting Gibson, and soon. Preferably in the same environment as the one where he'd left her sister.

From now on, she'd ensure that she carried Mace, along with the bottle of perfume and the personal alarm she always carried in her designer handbags. Fiona picked up the menu from the table. "Let's order dinner and open a bottle of wine, eh?"

"I might manage a little. Why don't you and Ami order, and I'll have a little of each of your meals? They're always huge portions, anyway—too big for one person."

"Ami, have you decided what you're going to have yet?" Fiona called out, picking up the phone, ready to dial and place the order.

A red-eyed Ami came back into the room and collapsed on the sofa beside Linda. "I couldn't eat anything. Linda, I'm so sorry."

The two sisters exchanged puzzled glances, and then eyed their flatmate with concern. Ami was such a sensitive soul. Linda's attack had hit her hard.

Fiona put the phone back in its docking station and sat down beside Ami. She threw an arm around her friend's shoulders and hugged her. "It's all right, Ami. Linda will be fine, eventually. I'll make sure of that. There's no need for any of us to worry. We'll all watch out for each other. Buck up, sweetie."

Ami looked at both of them and gave a simple nod. "I'm being silly. It's Linda we need to take care of."

Fiona searched deep into the Chinese girl's tiny black eyes and spotted something she hadn't noticed before. She had no idea what that something was, but right then wasn't the right time to delve further. Maybe Ami had been abused before and wasn't sure how to share it, maybe she was devastated by what Linda had gone through and simply didn't know how to show her how much she cared. Either way, Fiona had a feeling that the three of them would be crawling over eggshells for a while, not wishing to upset each other.

Fiona also realised that it would be up to her to make sure everyone recovered from the trauma and the undeniably fraught emotions. She had to come up with a plan that would help all of them get their lives back on track, and fast.

Eventually, the three of them decided they would indeed split two meals between the three of them. Fiona placed the order for a chicken tikka and a chicken korma. While they waited for the food to arrive, Ami poured them each a glass of Chablis.

When the doorbell rang about forty minutes later, both Ami and Linda jumped up in the air.

"Calm down, you two. It'll be the delivery guy." Despite her reassuring words, Fiona still checked who was at the door through the spyhole before she opened it. Crumbs, Fi. You're getting as nervy as the others.

That was when the idea came to her. She knew exactly how to bring safety and security back into the flatmate's world, but the idea would need thorough examination before she acted upon it.

The evening remained subdued, and the girls went to bed early. However, they each checked that the safety chain was securely fastened before turning in for the night.

Once in bed, Fiona shuddered at the thought of living the rest of her life in fear and spent the next few hours going through the local paper, searching for an ad that would help put her safety plan into action.

On the penultimate page, she found the very ad she was looking for. She picked up the pen from the bedside table beside her and circled the ad several times. Then, she turned off the light and snuggled under the quilt, smiling as part one of her new plan slotted into place.

Now all she had to do was ring her boss and arrange yet another day off.

CHAPTER FOUR

Another Indian summer morning streamed through the curtains. Lorne jumped out of bed before Tony pounced on her as he usually did first thing.

"Do you want to go in the garden, boy?" she asked Henry. The spritely dog was already halfway down the stairs before she'd stepped off the first step. She opened the kitchen door and held onto his collar. "No chasing the chickens, you hear me? We need their eggs for breakfast, and if you keep chasing them, they'll give up laying."

Henry whined a little before she set him free. Lorne watched the dog immediately run after the black cockerel that had his chest puffed out and was in the middle of his dawn alarm call. The cockerel half ran and half flew across the yard and leapt over the chicken-wired enclosure where the other birds were pecking around disinterested, before Henry had the chance to sink his teeth in to his rump.

Lorne laughed, then stretched. She walked through the back door and filled the kettle, ready for her morning cup of coffee.

A few minutes later, a sleepy Tony joined her in the kitchen. He snuck up behind her and enveloped her in his strong arms. "Morning, Mrs. Warner."

She turned to face him. It didn't matter how many times she heard the name—it still sent a tiny ripple of excitement through her. "Morning, Mr. Warner. Sleep well?"

He screwed up his nose and tilted his head from side to side. "So-so. The leg was giving me jip during the night."

The doctor had told them that despite Tony's leg being amputated at the knee, it wasn't uncommon to still have sensations where the missing limb used to be.

"Sorry to hear that, love. I wonder how long that's going to take to wear off." She placed her arms around the back of his neck.

He kissed the top of her forehead. "Not sure. Never mind. Hey, what's on the agenda today?"

That was Tony all over—never one to wallow in self-pity, always keen to move the conversation away from his disability.

Lorne traced a finger down his cheek. "I thought I'd spend some time with Hercules today. I put him in the stable last night. I'd like to get him used to being in the paddock as soon as possible, but I'm not sure what his reaction is going to be."

"Poor sod. He's probably never seen daylight before. I nearly thumped his owner yesterday when he was offloading him. As he walked him around the side of the trailer, he whacked the poor bugger in the side with a stick—at least, I think he did. I followed them round. I heard the thwack but couldn't be a hundred percent sure what had happened. You don't have to be Einstein to figure it out though, do you?"

"What? You should've told me."

"What and risk you being done for assault?"

Lorne, smiled. "It would've been worth it. Anyway, I doubt an assault on an animal abuser would have any legs in court, if you'll pardon the pun. I hope Hercules settles in okay. If not, I've heard of this woman in Maidstone who's a kind of horse whisperer."

Tony groaned and turned his attention to making the coffee.

She swiped him on the arm. "Hey, what's wrong with that?"

"Your father warned me about your fascination with whisperers. Henry was brought up under Cesar Millan's guidance, wasn't he?"

Lorne pulled a face and poked her tongue out at him. "Yes, he was, and he's a perfect specimen of a well-balanced, well-behaved dog despite all the negative media Cesar has had recently."

"Try telling that to the cockerel he just tried plucking," Tony said, laughing.

As if on cue, Henry pushed open the back door, stood in the doorway, and barked at Tony.

Lorne swiped her husband's head for the second time that morning and said out of the corner of her mouth, "Shhh... He's perceptive. He understands every word you say."

"He does, huh? Hey boy, supercalifragilisticexpialidocious!"

Lorne watched with amusement as the dog cocked his head, turned, and walked back out into the yard. "You're wicked. What's he ever done to you?"

"I know, but I love winding him up. Getting back to today's duties, what do you have planned for me today?"

"I thought you and Dad could make a start cutting down some of the trees in the far field. The wood will need to be stacked for a year or two before we can use it on the fire, but that'll save you a job, next spring."

Tony contemplated the task for a short while. "Ahh, I get it. Typical Lorne, always thinking ahead. You mean it'll be less work to do if and when the PI business gets going."

She chuckled. "There was a reason why you were an MI6 agent. There's no fooling you, is there, mister?"

Tony gave her his best schoolboy grin as her father joined them. "Coffee, Dad?"

"Please, love. So I'm going to be adding woodcutter to my C.V., am I?"

"If that's all right, Dad. There's not a lot else to do today. Although that could change at any moment, the rate the rescue calls have been coming in lately. I'm off to take a shower." She handed her father a mug of coffee and set off up the stairs.

When she came out of the bathroom, Tony was sitting on the end of the bed waiting for her. "What's the next step regarding the business, then? The PI business, I mean."

After towel-drying her shoulder-length hair, she threw the towel in the Ali-baba basket in the corner and joined her husband on the bed. "Run an ad in the local paper, I suppose. Pete used to have a connection with a guy at the local rag. I'll see if I can track him down." Mentioning her former partner's name filled her with a moment's sadness.

Tony rested his hand on her bare leg, where her towelling robe had separated. "You okay?"

She leaned over and kissed him on the cheek. "Yeah, I'm fine. I know it's silly, but sometimes I swear I can feel him around me. Hear his laughter when something disastrous happens. Is that crazy?"

"Yes and no. You two were very close. While I wouldn't admit it to everyone, I think my ex-colleagues—you know, the ones that have been killed in the line of duty—have helped me out in certain situations in the past."

"Really?" Lorne had never expected to hear such a confession leave her husband's lips. She no longer felt silly, feeling the way she did about Pete's sustained involvement in her life.

"Not sure I would've made it out of Afghanistan if I hadn't had a divine intervention or two."

"You're probably right. That must have been an horrendous time. I'm so glad you're not putting your life on the line any longer."

Tony stood up and smiled down at her. "I take it you haven't seen me handling—or mishandling—a chainsaw yet?"

Lorne laughed as he disappeared into the bathroom.

Once dressed, Lorne fed Henry his first meal of the day, then set off to feed the other inmates, as she liked to call them. The dogs in the kennels welcomed her with wagging tails and lots of excited barks. One by one, she took them out of the kennels and let them run around the exercise compound Tony and Lorne created so the dogs could stretch their legs a few times each day, rather than be cooped up in their kennels hour upon hour with little human contact.

Lorne's favourite was a big brute of a black and tan German shepherd. Blackie had been with them a little over a month, after her father found him wandering the streets. The dog had been skin and bones, looked like he hadn't had a meal in weeks, let alone a decent one. The vet had put Blackie at a three on the chart of malnourishment, with one being at death's door.

She had taken Blackie back for a check-up last week, and the vet had been both delighted and astonished by the dog's remarkable progress. It hadn't taken much to get the dog back in shape—two meals a day, and a groom or two from Charlie, when she was around.

Lorne knew the dog wouldn't be around for long. She already had a few enquiries about him but if she'd learnt anything from rescuing dogs from Sheila, her mentor who ran P.U.P.S., it was how important it was to make sure a proper home visit was carried out before rehoming a dog. Fences needed to be secure, gardens free of suspect obstacles—and an owner's lifestyle was also taken into consideration before Lorne handed over one of her dogs. If all the criteria weren't fully met, then there was the likelihood of the dogs being returned to her, and that wouldn't be fair to the animals.

She'd just finished exercising all the dogs—and could hear the drone of the chainsaw working in the distant fields—when a car pulled up in the back yard. Tony had placed a sign at the front of the property for customers to come round back. There was always one of them around doing one chore or another.

The car was a flashy MR2 sports car. Out stepped a tall blonde woman, dressed in designer jeans tucked into high-heeled cowboy boots. She pushed her sunglasses into her hair and looked around her. Was that disgust on her face?

Warily, Lorne approached the woman with an outstretched hand. "Hi, I'm Lorne. Can I help you?"

The woman looked down her nose at Lorne's hand and refused to shake it. "I'm looking for the owner."

Wiping her hands on the back of her jeans, Lorne said, "You've found her."

The woman's whole demeanour changed. Her expression softened into an embarrassed smile, and her uptight tone changed into one she probably used on a sick old relative. "Please, forgive my rudeness. It's been a tense week."

Lorne's detective antenna shot up and started probing the air for more juicy titbits. "That's okay." She held her arms out to the side and looked down at her messy clothes. "Sorry, it goes with the territory, I'm afraid. You should've been around here yesterday, when my husband tried to have a bath in some mud, and muggins here had to rescue him."

The woman laughed. "Glad I missed that particular episode of 'down on the farm.' I'm Fiona Carter, by the way. I saw an advert in the Kent Advertiser about this place. I'm after a dog."

"I see. I'm afraid we don't have any small dogs lodging with us at the moment," Lorne replied, thinking the woman was after one of those furry rats, draped in a diamond-studied collar, which top models carry around in their handbags—their very expensive handbags.

Fiona rolled her eyes in amusement. "I'm after the opposite, actually. I need a guard dog type, not a yapper. Do you have any here?"

Lorne studded the woman, then her car. "You know I have to carry out home checks? To make sure the owners and the dogs are a perfect match."

"I appreciate that." The woman followed her gaze. "Ah, I know the car doesn't seem very practical. I room with a couple of girlfriends, and nine times out of ten, there's always someone at home, so the dog would be walked every day."

Lorne nodded. Still trying to dissuade the woman who didn't look in the least like a dog lover, she said, "He'll need access to a garden. Large dogs need equally large gardens to exercise in. Do you have one of those?"

"Yep, we live in a flat which has its own garden. The other tenants don't have access to it, so that shouldn't be a problem."

"I take it the garden is secure?"

Fiona nodded firmly. "It is. Can I take a look at the dogs?"

Happy that the woman didn't appear to be put off by Lorne's excuses why she shouldn't have a dog, she said, "Of course. I'm so sorry. I used to be a detective, and it's hard to ditch the interrogation mode. I think I have just the dog for you. How do you feel about GSDs?"

They headed towards the kennels.

Frowning, Fiona asked, "GSDs? You've lost me."

"Sorry. German shepherds. Some people have an aversion to them. Blackie is as soft as they come."

The women's frown deepened, and Lorne couldn't help wondering why. "Something wrong?"

"Not exactly. Umm... I was after a guard dog, really. The more ferocious the better."

"To be honest, I doubt you'd be able to cope with a proper guard dog. They're mostly undomesticated and don't tend to make good house pets." Lorne carried on walking in the direction of the kennels, and the woman followed her. She was dying to know why the woman was interested in getting a guard dog, but she fought hard not to ask the obvious question. Maybe she would ask if the option of a home check ever arose.

The decibels flew off the scale when the two women entered the row of thermostatically controlled, heated indoor kennels. "Sorry. I suppose I should supply ear muffs for my visitors."

Fiona waved a hand in front of her as her eyes sought out Blackie, who was standing in the middle of his six-foot-square kennel, barking at them.

"Blackie, meet Fiona Carter. I'll get him out, and you can get more acquainted with him in the compound."

Although Fiona smiled at her, Lorne suspected the woman was slightly apprehensive of the dog.

Retrieving the lead off the rack at the end of the kennel, Lorne told her, "Please, don't worry. He's a gentle giant, you'll see. Have you ever owned a dog before?"

"Years ago. My parents always had labs when we were growing up."

"The breeds are very different. Blackie came to us about a month ago. Painfully thin and covered in a sticky stuff that resembled tar. My dad found him wandering around near the rubbish bins at the local supermarket, scavenging for food."

Fiona gasped. "But that's awful. Look at him. He's beautiful."

"He is now, thanks to the love and care he's received here. I'd hate for Blackie to go backwards. It's important that anyone taking him on recognises the pitfalls of having a large breed."

Fiona nodded and looked at Lorne. "You've done a remarkable job with him. If I take him home with me, I can assure you the girls would love him as much as me. He'd be spoilt rotten."

Lorne cringed at Fiona's last sentence. Why did everyone who took in a rescue dog think they had to spoil it? "A word of warning: It's just as easy to kill dogs through kindness as through abuse. Many people feel the need to give their dogs human food—you know, the odd digestive biscuit or two. They don't seem to appreciate how damaging that can be to their pets."

Fiona nodded her understanding and repeated her assurance, "I can assure you, if I take Blackie on, he'll be treated as a dog and given only dog food and dog treats."

Lorne opened the kennel and attached the lead to Blackie's collar. Fiona followed Lorne and the dog outside. Once Blackie was unleashed, he went up to Fiona and sniffed first her boots, then her jeans, his tail wagging the whole time he investigated his prospective new mistress.

The young woman appeared to be surprisingly at ease with the dog. Most people were initially apprehensive about meeting the larger breeds. Fiona crouched down to pet the shepherd, and he licked the side of her face. She giggled and almost toppled backwards.

"Well, you two seem to have hit it off. He likes playing fetch with a tennis ball, by the way." Lorne went in search of the ball near the link fencing. She threw the ball, and the dog immediately ran after it.

He came to a screeching halt, retrieved the ball, and trotted back to them with the ball in his mouth. When he reached them, he sat and dropped the ball at Fiona's feet.

"Good boy," she said, picking up the wet ball and throwing it to the back of the compound.

Lorne produced a tissue from her jeans pocket and offered it to Fiona. She waved it away and immediately went up in Lorne's estimation.

The game continued for the next ten minutes, until Blackie headed for the door to the kennel.

Lorne laughed. "I think you've succeeded in wearing him out. He's still a little unfit. He'll get there, though."

They followed Blackie inside the kennel.

"Gosh, I never thought. Sorry. So, what's the next step? You, coming out to do the home visit?" Fiona patted the dog between the ears.

Lorne filled up his water bowl and shut the kennel door. "That's right. If we go in the house, I can check the diary, to see when it would be convenient for us both."

Before they reached the house, Fiona said, "I was kind of hoping you could come out today. I've got the day off work, you see."

"Wow, when you get an idea in your head, you certainly like to run with it, don't you?"

"All my friends say the same thing. I'm the same at work. No half-measures for me."

Lorne flipped open the diary to see if she could possibly move the afternoon's appointments around a little. Two of the appointments were visits from the local RSPCA, who had a few dogs they needed temporary homing for the next few weeks until they had room at the local pound. Then there were a few visits booked in for people wanting to rehome a staffy and a collie.

Lorne figured that if she spoke to Tony nicely enough, he could handle the appointments for her while she visited Fiona's flat. It would be nice to see Blackie settled into a new home as soon as possible. "I'll need to ask hubby if he can do me a favour, but I can't see any reason why I can't call round and see you about four. How's that?"

Fiona didn't hesitate answering, "That's great. The other girls should be back around then, too."

"Excellent. I can't wait to meet them." Lorne handed Fiona a notebook and pen, asked her to jot down her address, then saw the young woman out to her MR2, which was sitting in the yard, glittering in the sun.

After waving Fiona off, Lorne went in search of Tony and her father in the bottom field.

"Damn thing! What is the matter with it?" Tony cursed. He was bent over the chainsaw, pulling the starter cord trying to make it spark into life.

"I think it's time we got a new one. I told you not to trust that bloke at the second hand shop."

Tony looked up and glared at her. "I'll take it back this afternoon. If he can't fix it, he can bloody well give me my money back."

"Ah, can you take it in early? I've just made an appointment for late afternoon, and I was hoping you'd take care of the appointments already booked in." She gave him her broadest smile and fluttered her eyelashes the way she always did when she really wanted to wrap him around her finger.

Tony shook his head in dismay, and her father burst out laughing. "Look, why don't I deal with the appointments? That leaves Tony free to sort the chainsaw out. It'll be good practice for me."

"What? You mean you'll take care of things round here for me, Dad?" Lorne went to hug him, but he stepped back.

"On the understanding that you two help me out in the mornings and evenings," her father said, looking first at Lorne and then at Tony for agreement.

"You bet. Instead of getting up at seven, I'll set the alarm for six. That'll be all right, won't it, love?" she asked Tony, who was looking at her as if she'd just dealt him a Tyson-like punch to the stomach.

"Like I have a choice in the matter?" he mumbled, and he turned his attention back to the reluctant piece of machinery.

"Anyway, Dad. I should imagine most of our work will happen in the evening or during the night. But you have my word that we'll muck in when we can. Come on, Henry. We have work to do." Lorne skipped away, with Henry trotting along beside her.

The rest of the morning was spent cleaning out and feeding the animals. She'd dropped in to see Hercules in his temporary stable. He appeared to be so much happier with life now; his head was upright, and he seemed to be taking far more interest in surroundings.

Lorne noticed the little feral cat they'd inherited when they had purchased the farmhouse, curled up asleep on the straw behind Hercules. Gratitude seeped through her. It was strange how animals knew when others needed company and guidance.

With the sun's rays already beating down, Lorne decided that she wouldn't let Hercules out into his paddock until the evening, when it would likely be much cooler. She didn't want the little donkey having any adverse effects from the relatively new experience. It would be best if he got used to being outside slowly and in his own time.

She went over to the string bag in the corner of the barn, took out a large carrot, and offered it to Hercules. At first, he appeared hesitant, as if he didn't really know what to make of the long orange pointed vegetable, which broke Lorne's heart. Then, with a little encouragement, he nibbled at the end, liked the taste, and ended up munching his way through it in seconds.

After preparing bacon sandwiches for the two men in her life, Lorne attacked the few bits of paperwork she had to deal with, mainly suppliers' bills that needed paying.

Then she changed into a summer dress that she hadn't worn in ages and set off in the van to Fiona's flat.

CHAPTER FIVE

Lorne eased through the thickening mid-afternoon traffic and arrived at the flat, which was situated in a respectable neighbourhood on the outskirts of Gravesend, about twenty minutes after leaving her place.

The flat was part of an old Victorian house. Lorne rang the doorbell to the first flat. An abrupt voice came out of the metal speaker. "Yes? Who is it?"

Lorne pressed the button and spoke into the mic grill. "It's Lorne Simpkins. I've come to see Fiona."

"Of course. Push the door and come through," the voice ordered.

The door clicked, and Lorne entered a communal hallway. Fiona was holding a door open to the flat on the ground floor. "Hi. Come in."

Lorne squeezed past her and stepped into a large lounge. On the sofa was a petite Chinese girl who had a pile of books beside her and an A4 notebook balancing on her lap. She looked up and smiled shyly at Lorne.

"This is Ami." Fiona knocked softly on the door behind her. "Linda, the lady is here to see us."

Fiona pointed at a rocking chair, indicating where she wanted Lorne to sit. "Do you mind if I see the garden first?" Lorne asked, looking through the coloured voile curtain to the garden beyond.

"Good idea." Fiona pulled back the French door, and they both wandered outside onto a patio area that had a gas barbecue on one side, and a table and four chairs on the other.

The garden impressed Lorne. "Wow! What is this, about eighty feet?"

Fiona smiled. "I guess so. We have a man come in every week to cut the grass and generally keep it tidy. I had a quick look around when I came back. I spotted a small area at the rear that could be deemed a little dubious. I'll show you."

They walked down the path that had grass on either side, and a few evergreen shrubs dotted the area, with no flowers as such. They reached the rear fence.

Lorne wobbled the fence panel and noted how rickety it was. Moving down to the bottom, she pushed and pulled at it. The panel appeared to be broken or rotten at one edge. "Hmm... I'd say this needs replacing rather than repairing. Could your maintenance man do that?"

"No problem. I'll get it fixed ASAP. As you can see, we don't really do flowers, so Blackie won't be shouted at all the time to keep off the beds. He'll be free to go wherever he likes. That's if we have him."

"Okay, provided this panel is fixed, I'm satisfied that Blackie or another dog would enjoy this garden and be safe running around out here. All right if I have a chat with your other flatmates now?"

"Sure. Can I get you a coffee or tea?"

They entered the lounge just as another girl came out of the room Fiona had tapped on before.

Lorne found it hard to hide her shock at the young woman's appearance. "My God, are you all right?"

Fiona rushed to help the girl onto the sofa. The poor girl looked very uneasy walking, as if she could faint at any moment. "This is my sister Linda. She's had a bit of an ordeal lately. You're getting better though, aren't you, love?"

Lorne couldn't stop staring at the young woman, at the appalling bruises covering her face and the fact that her ankle was in a cast. She knew it was rude of her to stare, and had she still been in the Met, she would have been called unprofessional by her colleagues, but the girl's injuries were like a magnet to Lorne.

Linda swallowed hard before she gave a weak smile. "Hi, I'm sorry to alarm you. I'm getting there."

"Please forgive my rudeness. I don't mean to stare, but... What the hell happened?"

Fiona patted her sister's hand and went into the kitchen to boil the kettle. No one answered until Fiona returned. "Linda had a bit of a mishap the other night."

A mishap! "Wow, some mishap," Lorne tried to answer matter-of-factly, but the words didn't come out as lightly as she'd intended.

The woman was beaten black and blue. Lorne surmised that either Linda was involved with an abusive partner, or she had been assaulted by a stranger. Lorne figured the latter scenario was probably the more accurate one, as Fiona hadn't mentioned any men sharing the flat with them.

Linda started crying. Fiona rushed to her side, while Ami's attention dropped into her studies once more. The room suddenly felt uncomfortable to Lorne.

Fiona shrugged at Lorne as she comforted her sister. "I'm sorry. Maybe we could do this another time?"

Lorne nodded, stood up, and prepared to leave.

"No. Wait. Give me a minute, and I'll be fine. I don't want you to have a wasted trip," Linda said between sniffs.

Lorne reached into her briefcase and took out the checklist Sheila had suggested she devise for the home visits. "If you're sure?"

Both Linda and Fiona nodded before Fiona got up to finish making the coffee.

"Okay, so you both know that Fiona came to see me today with regard to rehoming a dog in my care. I have to ask if you're all in agreement with that decision?" Lorne looked over at Linda, who was nodding frantically. Out of the corner of her eye, she saw Ami give the briefest of nods, as though she was doubtful about the idea. "Ami, do you have any reservations?"

The girl glanced up at Lorne. She appeared uncertain about what to say in front of Linda. Reluctantly, she said, "I guess."

Fiona came back in to the room carrying a tray with four mugs on it. Lorne noticed the hard stare Fiona gave Ami as she put the tray down on the coffee table.

Ami's cheeks flushed. "I mean, yes. It's okay with me."

Hmm... Lorne was far from satisfied. Nevertheless, she pressed on with the checklist, deciding to voice any doubts she might have at the end. "I've gone over a few issues in the garden that need addressing with Fiona. Providing they are corrected, I can't see any problems. Can I ask what type of dog you all have in mind?"

"I've told them what a darling Blackie is and that I think he would be an ideal dog for us, and we're all in agreement, aren't we girls?"

Lorne carefully watched Ami's reaction. She didn't think the girl oozed a great amount of certainty. "Ami?"

Ami looked at her flatmates, placed the books she had on her lap on the floor beside her, and stood up. "I said, I'm okay with it," she snapped before she stomped out of the room.

Lorne looked over at Fiona, whose expression was twisted in anger.

Sighing, Lorne shuffled her papers and put them back in her bag. "I think you still have a lot of talking to do on the subject. Maybe it would be better if you rang me next week with your decision."

Fiona held up a hand. "Please don't go. Ami will be fine with whatever we decide."

Lorne shook her head. "I'm sorry, Fiona. I only have the dog's welfare at heart here. If there is a possibility of him not being wanted or liked, then I'll have to find him somewhere else."

Linda's hand shot out and grabbed her sister's arm tightly. "You have to let us have the dog."

Raising a questioning eyebrow, Lorne asked, "Why do I have to, Linda?"

The sisters stared long and hard at each other before Fiona spoke. "If we don't get a dog then we'll be on tenterhooks. Scared of every knock on the door. Afraid to go out. We're living under a threat."

"A threat?" Lorne queried.

"That's right." Fiona hesitated as if afraid to say the words out loud. "You see, Linda was raped, and her attacker has threatened to come after me."

CHAPTER SIX

Lorne was rendered speechless for a few mind-numbing seconds. When she finally recovered, she asked gently, "Did you know the man?" In her experience, nine out of ten women were raped by men they were acquainted with.

Ashamed, Linda looked down at her hands, which were clasped tightly together in her lap. "I did. He wasn't a friend, but I do know him. He's a frequent visitor to the same club I go to every week."

"Did you notify the police, Linda?"

"Yes. They carried out a rape kit, but he used a condom," she replied, defeated.

Damn. Without semen, the police would have little to go on, unless... "I see, but you gave the police his name, didn't you?"

Linda turned to look at her sister and frowned.

"Lorne used to be a detective. It's okay to answer her questions, love. It might be good to get a female officer's perspective on things," Fiona reassured her sister.

Lorne smiled. "Former female officer. Can I ask how the police have handled the attack? I mean, how they're proceeding with the case? You did give the police his name, didn't you?" she repeated. She took out a spare sheet of paper and started jotting down notes as Linda answered her questions.

The three of them almost jumped out of their seats when the doorbell rang. "I'll get it," called Ami, already on the way to the front door.

Linda cleared her throat and went over what had happened at the station. At least, she started to before a smartly dressed man in his early thirties barged into the room.

An embarrassed Ami trailed behind him. "I'm so sorry. I tried to tell him you were busy, but..."

Fiona leapt out of her seat and stood between the man and her sister. Lorne remained seated and observed the situation with interest. "Jason. What in God's name are you doing here?"

The man appeared bewildered. Changing expressions swept across his face. Confusion settled on his features as he pulled Fiona to the side and glanced down at Linda. "Christ! It doesn't matter what I'm doing here. What happened to Linda?"

Linda hid her face in her hands as Fiona grabbed the man by the arm and steered him through to the bedroom. "I won't be a sec!" she shouted at the perturbed threesome left behind.

"He's her boyfriend," Linda enlightened Lorne.

"Oh, right. I take it he wasn't aware of...what's taken place?"

Ami sat on the sofa next to Linda and clutched her shaking hand. "Don't be frightened. Fiona will calm him down. I'll stay with you until they're finished."

Lorne jotted down the name of the policeman who had interviewed Linda, appalled that a female officer hadn't been involved in the interview process. Linda told her that the officer concerned was supposed to have visited the offender the evening before, but she had no idea how things had turned out, as no one from the station had contacted her since. They continued speaking despite the sound of raised voices coming from the bedroom.

The ruckus was affecting Linda, so Lorne tapped on the bedroom door. When Fiona opened it, her cheeks were beet red, and her eyes were wide with fury.

"Sorry to disturb you, I'm almost done here, but I thought you should know that the shouting isn't helping Linda's state of mind."

Fiona rolled her eyes as if she hadn't realised the others could hear what was being said in the bedroom. "I'm sorry. I'll be with you in a minute."

The woman shut the door in Lorne's face before she had a chance to say anything further. For Linda's sake, Lorne sat down again, even though she had already decided this would not be an ideal home for Blackie. She did, however, feel sorry for the way Linda had been treated and wanted to give her as much support as she could.

As Linda retold the harrowing events, Fiona ushered Jason through the living room and out to the front door. She returned a few minutes later, full of apologies. "He was annoyed I stood him up last night and, as he couldn't get hold of me at work today, the idiot thought I had another man here. I put him straight on that one. Sorry, where were we?"

"Actually, I must be getting back. Linda, here's my home number. If I can help in some small way, then don't hesitate to get in touch. "I'll let you know what I decide about Blackie next week." Lorne shook hands with everyone, and Fiona saw her to the front door.

Fiona held the door open. "Any idea what day?"

"I just need to dot a few I's, et cetera. By Wednesday, if I can."

"Why don't you just come out and say it, Lorne. You're going to reject us, aren't you?" Fiona asked sharply, cocking an expectant eyebrow.

Lorne looked at the traffic behind her as she tried to conjure up a suitable excuse. She thought honesty would be the safest route to take, after all the girls had been through. "To be honest, I think you want a dog for the wrong reasons. While I completely understand and sympathise with your situation, I feel I can't place a dog in this environment. In a few months, maybe when things have settled down, you'll understand my decision. A dog needs love and care from day one, and I just think the three of you have too much anxiety and anger surrounding you at the moment. It wouldn't be fair on either side."

"Fair enough. If that's your decision, I'll go elsewhere for a dog. Whether we get one from you or someone else, Mrs. Warner, there will be a dog in this house by the weekend. Goodbye."

The harsh words were followed by the oak door being shut in Lorne's face. Charming! Goodbye to you, too.

During the drive home, she blocked out the usually noisy sound of the van and mulled over Linda's nightmarish predicament. Hmm... Maybe I should give Katy a call to ask her to do some digging on this chap for me. See what she can come up with. Men like that shouldn't be allowed to get away with rape just because he put a plastic sock on his willy before doing the deed.

Once an idea started to fester, Lorne had to jump on it. She pulled over into the nearest lay-by and dialled Katy's mobile. "Hey, you. How's it going?"

"Just a minute. I'll go into my office. Hey, how are you?"

Lorne laughed. It was good to talk to her old-young partner again. "I asked first."

"Oh, you know. Fair to middling. This place isn't the same without you biting our heads off."

"You cheeky mare. How are things going with AJ?"

"Slowly. We said we'd take things steady until we're sure that Darren isn't going to bother me anymore."

"Has he been hanging around again?" Lorne asked, concerned.

"Not since he wrecked my flat, but you never know. I'd like to leave it a year or so before I get involved with someone again.

Anyway, there are our jobs to consider. Neither AJ nor I want to move away from the team. It's a productive team which gets results. We'd be daft to throw that away. How are things 'down on the farm'?" Katy asked in the worst Devonshire accent Lorne had ever heard.

"Was that your attempt at Welsh?" she teased. "Things are going great, but I have a surprise for you."

"You're not...?"

Lorne tutted, reading her former partner's mind. "Give me a break, will you? Charlie's more than any mother can handle. She'd try any supermum's patience. Actually, I'm being a tad unfair. She's been as good as gold for months now. Not sure what she's after; I'm sure I'll find out soon. No, I'm branching out."

"How can a rescue shelter branch out?" Katy asked, confused.

"Not with this business. I'm starting up another one."

"Oh, I see. So you'll have two rescue centres on the go. How will that work out?"

Lorne let out an exasperated breath. "No, you don't see at all. I'm going to become a PI." There was silence on the other end of the phone. "Katy? Are you there?"

"Yeah, I'm just trying to work out what the initials mean. Puppy institution or something?"

Another long breath seeped through her lips. "A private investigator, numpty!"

Then there was nothing, zip, no response whatsoever from Katy, prompting Lorne to ask, "Katy? You still there?"

A long whistle greeted her. "Jeez, what can I say? A PI. Who'd have thunk it?"

Lorne laughed. "Yeah, I know it's a bit insane. But I figured I'd be my own boss and I wouldn't be jumping through hoops for bosses who don't appreciate me."

"Well, there is that, I suppose. What sort of cases will you be focusing on?"

"Whatever comes our way to start with. We'll see how things pan out from there."

"I have to say I admire you, but then that's nothing new. When is all this starting up?" Katy asked, sounding more interested than Lorne had anticipated.

"My diploma came in the post this morning, then the weirdest thing happened."

"You get a diploma? Lorne, weird has a way of always finding its way to your door."

She chuckled. "Yeah, I know. Look, before I go any further, I was wondering if you'd be able to work with me at all. You know, if a case comes in and I need a background check running on a suspect. Although I wouldn't want you getting into bother for it."Katy went quiet for a second or two. "Not sure. You know I would if I could. Maybe we should see what Roberts has to say, first. You're his favourite DI—or former DI—after all, so I can't see any problems on that front. Can I get back to you later?"

Lorne bashed the steering wheel with her fist. She totally understood Katy's dilemma, but she had specifically rung up to get some information on Gibson. She guessed that would have to wait until Roberts gave the go ahead—if he gave the go ahead. She'd have to do her own mini background check on the 'net until Katy got back to her. "Okay, that's fair enough. Can you try to see him today?"

"It's nearly knocking off time. I'll see if I can grab him before he calls it a day. I'll ring you either later this evening or tomorrow."

"Thanks, mate. I better go before the traffic turns this road into a car park," Lorne said, turning the key in the ignition.

"Talk soon," Katy replied before she hung up.

CHAPTER SEVEN

Tony was waiting in the courtyard for her when she arrived home. His hair was damp from being in the shower. "Well?"

"The jury is still out. You look good enough to eat." Lorne got out of the car and hooked her arms around his neck and kissed him on the lips.

"Down, tiger. Your father is spying on us through the kitchen window. What happened? Wasn't the garden up to scratch?"

"No, that side of things was fine. I'm hungry. Let's eat, and I'll tell you all about it over dinner."

Tony raised a suspicious eyebrow and patted her on the bottom. "Hmm... Sounds ominous. Your dad is making beef and onion pie."

"Yum. Love Dad's pies."

After having a quick shower, Lorne joined her father and Tony at the kitchen table. Her father served the meal, and Tony poured them each a glass of red wine. She could get used to this, being waited on by two handsome men.

Two mouthfuls into the meal, Tony asked, "So? I'm dying to hear what went on."

Lorne gulped down the mouthful of delicious pie and, in-between mouthfuls, told Tony and her father how the visit had gone. They both remained silent until after she had finished telling her story.

"So they want the dog as a deterrent?" Tony asked.

"That's what it amounts to, yes," Lorne replied, wiping her mouth on the serviette and pushing her empty plate away. "That was scrummy, Dad. Thank you."

"My pleasure. Well, I can understand it from the women's point of view, but I also know that you will have the dog's interest to bear in mind, as well. Don't shout at me and let me finish before you react. Could you not give the girls a trial period with Blackie? A month, say?"

Lorne smiled at her ageing father, so wise and understanding in too many ways to mention. "On the journey back home, I was contemplating the same thing, Dad. I know it's against my better judgment, but if you could've seen the fear in all the girls' eyes. Actually, I'd like to offer them more help if I can."

"Uh-oh! I sense trouble brewing." Tony eyed her warily.

Lorne punched him gently on the top of the arm. "I'm worried about the condom aspect. Without evidence, it's going to be Linda's word against his. I need to spend some time on the computer tonight. I rang Katy on the way home—you know, to test the water. She's going to have a word with Roberts and get back to me with the outcome."

"This Linda, did she manage to scratch the bastard at all?" Tony asked.

Lorne started stacking the plates and took them over to the sink. "Nope. He tied her hands behind her back. Another reason why I think the police will also have their hands tied—excuse the pun. Anyone want some ice cream?"

"Not for me, love," her father said. "I'm thinking this guy has raped before."

Lorne nodded at her father. "I came to the same conclusion, Dad. To me, it sounded all planned out. From the innocent nod and joke sharing with the bouncer to being enticed to his home and being dumped back at the alley. I'll see what I can dig up on this Graham Gibson later. The police paid him a visit yesterday. When I last spoke to them, the girls had no idea of the outcome. I'll ring Fiona tomorrow to see what they had to say, if anything."

She took two dessert bowls from the cupboard and scooped two dollops of chocolate chip ice cream into each of them.

Tony took his bowl from Lorne. "I'll help later with the checking. Maybe—just maybe—if the coppers come up blank, we could make this our first case."

"You read my mind, although I haven't discussed it with the girls yet. Not sure they would be able to afford our fees."

Tony contemplated Lorne's words for a few minutes as he ate the ice cream on his spoon. "You could always do it pro bono. You know, to get you—or us, I should say—into the swing of things."

She looked over at her father for his opinion. He was nodding. "I'd do the same, if the police come back and say they're not willing to pursue the matter. Who's to say how many women he's raped? It has to stop or be stopped."

"Agreed. I'll be in the lounge, scouring the Internet for dirt on this Graham Gibson." Lorne rose from the table and walked towards the door.

"Umm... Aren't you forgetting something, dear wifey?"

She turned to face him and followed his gaze over to the pile of unwashed dishes. She pouted, and fluttered her eyelashes at him. "If you really and truly loved me, you would wash up while I got on with some real work. It's only a tiny bit."

Tony tutted. "Go on with you. I'll join in a little while, once I've done your chores."

"Thanks, sweetie," she called over her shoulder.

She opened the laptop on the coffee table and booted it up. A picture of Charlie cuddling Henry filled the screen. Lorne blew her daughter a kiss. "See you at the weekend, darling."

Once the computer had gone through the motions of starting up, Lorne typed "Graham Gibson" in the search engine. Several possible options appeared, but the girls had told her that the GG she was after worked in the city. She ran the pointer down the screen and located him. She selected his details and was taken to another screen.

Lorne enlarged the personal photo and studied it for a few minutes. Clean-shaven, close-cropped hair, looked like a model in one of those swanky aftershave ads off the TV, and dressed to impress in a beautifully cut business suit. His bottle green eyes sparkled with laughter, or was that mischievousness? Lorne had to admit that he didn't look like a rapist—but then, who did? It wasn't as if those guys ran around with the term rapist tattooed on their foreheads.

Wearing an arrogant sultry look and sporting perfect, blemish-free skin that screamed he religiously moisturised every morning and night, GG reminded her of a darker version of the footballer David Beckham. A shudder ran through her as she focused on his eyes, eyes that were purposefully angled so that he appeared to be looking through her and into her soul.

"There's something about you I don't like, sonny. Let's see what else we have on you." She tapped through another link highlighted on the screen, and it took her to the webpage of Domino Finances. At the top of the screen was a group photo of all the employees, and surprise, surprise: GG was posing in the centre at the front, a female colleague on either side of him.

Further investigation into Domino Finances led Lorne to a page full of satisfied customers singing their praises and a headline stating: "During troubled times, Domino Finances comes out on top for safe-guarding your money."

"How's it going?"

Lorne looked up and shrugged as Tony placed mugs of coffee on the table.

He sat on the couch beside her and she angled the computer so they could both see the screen.

"Have you come across this firm before?" Lorne asked.

"Can't say I have. That's a pretty impressive pedigree they have there, though. Their list of clients reads like a who's who of the finance world."

Lorne went back a few pages and showed Tony the picture she had found of GG.

"Is that him?" Tony scrutinised the picture through narrowed, untrusting eyes.

"Yeah, that's him. You should've seen what he did to Linda. In one way, I hope the police aren't able to proceed further, because I'd love to bring the smug-looking bastard to justice, myself."

Tony leaned over and kissed her temple. "Really? You do surprise me. Your paperweights have been lacking new additions lately. His balls would make a handsome addition."

Lorne smiled and returned to searching the Internet for anything dubious on the suspect, but unfortunately the results came back blank. "Damn, this guy looks cleaner than polished silver."

"Why don't you call it a day? Wait until you hear back from the girls and Katy, and then go from there, huh?" He pulled her back and slung a lazy arm over her shoulder.

"I guess that makes sense. If I don't hear from Fiona by noon tomorrow, I'll give her a call and tell her I've decided to place Blackie with them for a trial period. I'm sure they won't argue with that. Actually, after seeing what GG looks like, I'd feel much more comfortable if Blackie was there with them. I wouldn't be able to live with myself if anything further happened to either one of them."

Tony squeezed her shoulder. "The trouble with you is you have a soft centre. I know you want to take on the world and right all the wrongs in it, Lorne, but sometimes—just sometimes—even superheroes have to take a day off."

Their lips met in a lingering kiss.

"Have I told you lately how much I love you?" she asked, interlocking her fingers with his.

"Not since this morning, no."

CHAPTER EIGHT

Lorne was busy completing the paperwork she had started the day before when the house phone rang. "Hello?"

"Is that Lorne?"

She recognised the voice immediately. "Fiona?"

The woman sounded downhearted and sighed heavily. "I'm just ringing up to let you know that the police told us that they won't be taking any action against Graham Gibson."

Lorne thought as much. Not enough evidence. "Damn, I'm very sorry to hear that, Fiona. No point in me asking how Linda has taken the news."

"She's crumbled. Gone into her shell, and I'm not sure what I can do to snap her out of it."

"So what happens next?" Lorne asked, tidying some of the papers in front of her.

"I don't know. Is it so awful of me to want to stalk this guy and get revenge?"

"No. It's completely understandable, just not advisable. I do have a suggestion, though."

Fiona sighed on the other end of the line then said, "I'm listening."

"On the drive home I did a lot of thinking. Is it possible for me to bring Blackie over to meet the other girls, and we'll go from there?"

"Are you kidding? That'd be great, Lorne. I'd be so grateful to you." And she sounded it, too.

"That's only the beginning of what I have in store for you all. Will you all be at home today?"

Fiona remained quiet as she thought. "The only person I'm not sure about is Ami. Can you stay on the line while I text her?"

"Of course. I need to be sure Blackie feels at ease with you all, and vice versa."

Lorne heard the sound of Fiona's phone beeping an incoming text.

"Here she is. She'll be home at six this evening. Is that too late for you?"

It was really, after having to get up before the cock crowed, but Lorne didn't tell Fiona that. "That's fine. I'll bring Blackie, and we'll see how things go. Don't buy any food or anything like that. I'll supply what he needs for the next few days, just in case things don't work out."

"Are you sure? You really are too kind."

Lorne smiled as if Fiona was in the room with her. You think that's going to be the extent of my kindness? "We'll see you later. Give my regards to Linda, and tell her to keep her chin pointing upwards."

Lorne hung up and went in search of Tony. She found him with an axe trying to cut down the tree he'd started to annihilate the day before. By the look of things, the tree seemed to be fighting back. He had numerous scratches across the back of his hands and a raised red mark, approximately three inches long, on his left cheek.

"Baby, what happened?" She gently ran her finger down his cheek.

"This darn thing just doesn't want to come out. Maybe I'm not cut out to be a lumberjack."

"Let's get someone in. I wouldn't want that pretty face of yours to get all mashed up by the nasty tree." Tony already had a few scars on his face from his time as an agent. When they had first met, he had a pronounced, ugly scar on his right cheek, which had drawn her eye. That particular scar had faded well over the few years she had known him. But that was nothing to the permanent scars the Taliban had left him with on his chest and stomach. The Taliban had been brutal when they had tortured him, publicly flogging his front instead of his back. The bastards were always trying to figure out ways of upping the pain they dished out to their victims.

"We'll see. Maybe if the PI business takes off, we can consider hiring a full-time handyman, because I sense that all this land is going to be a full-time job to look after in itself."

"We'll see. Not regretting buying this place, are you?"

Tony mimicked the way her mouth had turned down and kissed the tip of her nose. "I'll be fine once I can get the hedges trimmed back. What's up, anyway? You're not your usual chirpy self."

"Fiona just rang. The police aren't interested in Linda's case."

"We thought that would happen. Did you tell her what your intentions were?" he asked, leaning on the axe in front of him.

"No. I'd like to see their faces when I do that. I just wanted to check if you had any plans for this evening. Only I said I'd drop Blackie off around six. I'd like to stay there a little while to help settle him in and talk over the PI aspect with the girls. That'd mean either an early or late dinner for you and Dad."

Tony shrugged. "Suits me. You could pick up fish and chips from the chippie on the way home."

She laughed. "You better get cracking and start burning off some excess calories, then."

Lorne spent the rest of the afternoon exercising the dogs, cleaning out the kennels, and gathering Blackie's food, bowls, and a selection of toys, getting him ready for his temporary home.

At five thirty, she and Blackie set off in the van to the girls' flat. She observed the dog in her rear-view mirror. He was panting excitedly, happy to be out of his kennel and eager to get to their destination. As she got the dog out of the van she said, "You'll be good, Blackie. For a few days, at least. Maybe longer, who knows?"

Lorne pushed the buzzer.

Fiona opened the door. The first thing she did was to crouch down and give Blackie some fuss, which was good to see, from Lorne's point of view. One down, two more to go.

Lorne handed the leash to Fiona and closed the front door behind her.

Linda approached the dog with a tiny bit of trepidation, but once the dog licked at the sores on her face, she fell in love with him.

Ami, however, was a different story altogether. Whether it was a cultural issue or something else, Lorne wasn't entirely sure. Didn't they eat dogs in China? Only that morning, Lorne had received a Facebook message from Charlie, urging her to sign a petition to put a stop to the fur farms in China, where the poor creatures lived their whole lives in cages and were skinned alive, then dumped on a heap to die the most horrific of deaths.

She shook the sickening image from her mind and continued to watch Ami's interaction—or lack thereof—with Blackie.

Fiona prompted Ami to stroke Blackie. "Go on, Ami. He won't hurt you."

Lorne wasn't keen on the idea of Ami being forced into something she didn't want to do. She walked over to stand beside Ami and beckoned the dog. She felt and sensed the fear emanating from the young woman. "Ami, can you look at me? It's obvious you're scared of Blackie. Give me your hands."

Ami looked at Lorne as if she had just escaped the local asylum.

Lorne smiled reassuringly as the other woman placed her hands lightly in hers. "Good. Now copy me. Breathe in deeply, and let it out extra slowly. Keep your gaze locked on mine."

Ami did as instructed. The intense anxiety the woman had been suffering from visibly slipped away.

That was, it slipped away until Blackie jumped up and hooked his paws over their arms. Ami squealed and ran to the sofa. Lorne hooked her fingers through Blackie's collar to prevent him from chasing Ami.

Fiona gave Lorne a look that asked 'How do we overcome that?'

The truth was, Lorne had no idea. She'd never met anyone with such an acute aversion to dogs before. She also knew that if Ami showed Blackie fear, he could react in one of two ways either by pestering her until she was forced to take notice of him or by acting aggressively, growling or attacking her, although Lorne doubted the latter scenario would be true of Blackie.

Lorne comforted the dog while Fiona settled on the sofa next to Ami to see what her problem was.

"I had no idea you didn't like dogs. Is there any way you'll try to get over your problem?" Fiona leaned in closer and whispered, "We need to show a united front, for Linda's sake. She needs to feel secure around here—we all do, hon."

Tiny tears dripped onto Ami's cheek. "I know, Fi, and I'm so sorry. But...dogs petrify me. I was bitten by one when I was a little girl. I can see Blackie is a nice dog, but my heart is pounding so hard just being in the same room with him. To be honest, I'm not sure I can cope with him living here with us."

"What are you saying? That you're not prepared to give it a try?"

"I didn't say that. But..." Ami refused to look up.

There was something more to her behaviour than she was willing to admit to. Lorne waited patiently as Fiona tried to encourage Ami to confide in her.

"Come on, Ami. For Linda's sake. Give Blackie a chance, at least for a few days."

Ami thought for a little while before she gave a brief nod.

But Lorne wasn't totally convinced that she was about to do the right thing, leaving Blackie with someone who appeared to be his prime carer, as both Linda and Fiona worked full time. Although, granted, Linda was off from work on the sick at the moment.

"Just to clarify the situation. Ami, once Linda goes back to work it'll be your responsibility to look after Blackie. To exercise, feed, and play with him, is that right?"

Ami shot Fiona a terrified look, then stood up and bolted into her bedroom.

"Ami..." Fiona called after her.

"Leave her, Fiona. I'm sure we'll find a way around this problem. Is she always so timid?"

"She's always been a quiet girl, but in the last month or so, she's been really different. We've been a bit worried about her. Since the attack, I'm afraid my primary concern has been Linda's welfare."

"How are you, Linda?" Lorne asked, smiling at the way the dog was looking up at her. He seemed happy in his new home, despite Ami's reluctance to make friends with him.

Ruffling Blackie between the ears, Linda replied, "Truthfully, I've had better days. I just can't understand why the police don't believe me. Do they think I did this to myself?" She pointed at the wounds on her face and wrists.

"I know how unfair it seems, Linda, but without any physical evidence—DNA, et cetera—their options are limited. Has the doctor said when you can go back to work?"

"In a day or two. I'm an estate agent. It's going to be hard for me to return to work. However, my boss is very understanding. He's told me I can stay in the office until I feel up to facing clients again or my ankle is out of plaster."

Satisfied that Linda was resigned to accepting the police decision not to go after Gibson, Lorne decided to broach the subject of her taking over the case. "Okay, here's where I stand on things: I'm willing to leave Blackie with you for a few days, as I've already stated. I do, however, have some concerns in regard to Ami's reaction to him. If that can be overcome in the near future, then I can see the arrangement becoming a permanent one."

Both Linda and Fiona looked relieved and in turn stroked the dog.

"I have something else—a proposition, if you like—to run past you both."

"Go on," said Fiona, her forehead furrowed.

"As you know, I used to be a detective. I retired from the force last year with the intention of concentrating on the animal rescue centre. Well, things have changed. I'm about to start up my own private investigation firm."

"Wow, how exciting for you," Fiona stated, admiration on her face.

"I hope so. Here's where you guys slot into the equation: I'd like you to be my first clients. Free of charge."

Astounded, Fiona dropped down onto the sofa, almost crushing Blackie in the process.

Linda cleared her throat. Her eyes misted over, she placed a hand to her breast. "You'd do that for me, for us?"

Lorne couldn't help feeling a little embarrassed by their reaction. "Linda, I believe in you. This guy needs to be caught and taken off the streets. He can't go on raping women and getting away with it. From what you've told me, I doubt you're the first or the last that he's lured away from that club."

From the doorway, they heard a sniffle, and a pained voice uttered, "You weren't."

CHAPTER NINE

The three of them turned to look at Ami, who, after voicing the words, had collapsed against the doorframe.

"Ami, what do you mean?" Lorne asked cautiously, hoping the girl wasn't about to say what she was thinking.

The girl stood unsteadily on her slim legs, and Lorne inched forward, ready to catch her if she fell.

"Linda's not the first."

"For God's sake, Ami, get on with it!" Fiona snapped. "What are you trying to tell us?"

Ami closed her eyes. Lorne lunged forward.

But the girl didn't fall. The only thing that fell were tears onto her cheek. "Gibson raped me, too."

Everyone else in the room gasped. It was a while before any of them found their voices.

Lorne guided the young woman to the end of the sofa and pushed her down. "Ami, when did this happen to you?"

Ami took a tissue from up the sleeve of her jumper and wiped her nose and eyes with it. "About a month ago."

"My God. Why didn't you tell us?" Fiona asked finally.

"I couldn't. I was so ashamed," she whispered, her head bowed with embarrassment.

Lorne placed a hand on Ami's shoulder. "Did you report it to the police, Ami?"

"No. I was too ashamed," she repeated.

A dumbfounded Linda said quietly, "But you don't or didn't have any injuries..."

"I know. I feel terrible, for not telling you, for not looking like you do."

Lorne had a feeling which way the conversation was going and interjected, "You don't have to apologise, Ami. When it happened, did you give in to him?"

"Yes. He's a powerful man. After he had finished, he spat on me like I was a piece of dirt."

Lorne squeezed Ami's shoulder and glanced up at the two sisters. Linda was staring at Ami with compassion and regret. Fiona on the other hand, looked as though she was capable of committing murder. Lorne couldn't decide if it was Gibson or Ami she wanted to kill.

"How could you?" Fiona screeched at her.

"Please, Fi, don't be cross with me," Ami pleaded, still unable to make eye contact with anyone.

"Don't be cross! How the fuck do you expect me to react? If you'd told us—either of us—this probably would never have happened to Linda! You do realise that, don't you?"

As Ami sobbed into the palms of her hands, Linda pulled on her sister's arm and shook her head. "Don't do this, Fiona. What good will it do? The damage is done now."

Fiona's eyes widened, and her fists clenched and unclenched by her sides. "I'm sorry, Linda. I can't and won't let this lie. She should've told us. I don't mean that Gibson attacked you but the fact that you were attacked at all. We could have helped you get over it. Do you agree, Lorne?"

Lorne cringed at being put on the spot. "Perhaps it would've been better in hindsight if you had confided in Linda and Fiona. It's not something you should have dealt with on your own. But what's done is done. I suggest we move forward, quickly."

"I'm sorry. Truly sorry," Ami muttered under her breath.

Fiona huffed, and Linda slapped her arm. "Fi, Ami was petrified. Unless you've been in that situation, you can't possibly know what it's like. Lorne, where do we go from here?"

Ami glanced up at Lorne and frowned.

"I'm just starting out as a private investigator, Ami. I've offered to look into Linda's case for free. With what you've just told us, I'd say it's imperative we get this guy off the street ASAP. I'll need you to help us, though. Are you up to that?"

"Anything. I'll do anything to help."

Lorne smiled and heard the two sisters breathe a heavy sigh of relief. "I'll need you to go to the police and inform them that Gibson raped you, too. Can you do that for me?"

Ami's chin dipped against her chest. Without looking at the others, she asked, "What good will it do?"

"I can understand your hesitation, but the more complaints the police have against Gibson, the better. They'll begin to take the case far more seriously."

Fiona shook her head. "I doubt that's going to happen. They'll probably think Ami is just making up another attack. You know, what with her living with us. Without any proof, I have a feeling they'll discount Ami's accusation from the outset."

Lorne nodded. "Fiona's right, but Ami, if you're willing to go through with it, I know from my experience in the force that Gibson's name will be put on a 'One to watch' list. If any other crimes similar to yours occur in the same area, his name will immediately be flagged."

"Oh, excellent. So all we have to do is wait for this scumbag to rape a few more women—then there's a chance he might be connected to all the crimes," Fiona stated, sarcasm evident in her tone.

Fiona had a point. No one knew better than Lorne how screwed-up the system was. That was why she had decided to branch out on her own, to right the wrongs that the police system couldn't or wouldn't do.

"I know it doesn't seem fair, Fiona, but that's the way it is. Now, about my proposal. I promise to give it my all. You have my word that if there is a way to get this guy, I'll find it. If you give me the chance, that is?" Lorne watched the uncertainty disappear from the three girls, to be replaced by hope. In unison, they all nodded.

"Okay. Here's what we do next: Ami, I need you to go to the police and give them a statement. Do you have a friend who could go with you?" Ami glanced at Fiona and Linda. "It would be better if it was a different friend—you know, because of the connection."

"I think my friend from uni will go with me."

"Great. Next, I need you, Linda, to tell me everything you know about Gibson. You said he had a girlfriend up till a few weeks ago. Any idea of her name?"

Linda shrugged, and her mouth twisted as she thought. "Not sure. The best I can do is ask around at the club, if I ever go back there."

"Don't worry, Linda. I'm not going to put you through that, although you shouldn't let this guy alter the way you live your life. If you do that, he's going to think he's won in more ways than one. I'll make enquiries at the club—discreet enquiries, especially as he appears to be well-known there."

"I understand, but it's going to be hard, venturing out at night again," Linda replied. Fiona patted her understandingly on the back of the hand.

"If we can go through a few details, Linda, I'll need to be getting back soon. Hubby will be expecting his dinner."

Over the next half an hour, Lorne jotted down four full pages of notes about Gibson, some of which even Ami provided. Lorne packed her pad away and handed Fiona a carrier bag containing everything she had brought with her for Blackie, essentials for a few days' stay.

"Are you sure about Blackie, Ami?" While taking notes, Lorne had noticed Ami getting nearer to the dog, intimating that she was willing to give him a chance.

"He seems a nice dog. Can I see how things go? All I can say is that I'll try my best with him, for all our sakes."

"I'm satisfied with that. He'll look after you—all of you. I'm confident of that." Lorne clicked her fingers, and Blackie rushed over to her. "Now you be a good boy and look after the nice ladies."

The dog licked her face, and she wiped her cheek on the sleeve of her coat. "Any problems—doesn't matter how insignificant you think they are—don't hesitate to contact me. In the meantime, I'll get started on your case. Hopefully, I'll be in touch in a few days. Look after each other."

Lorne left the room, and Blackie tried to follow until Linda caught him by the collar. Lorne heard the dog whimper slightly before the front door closed behind her. Unexpected tears welled up in her eyes. Sheila had warned her that she would need to harden up and to avoid getting attached to the dogs, but in Lorne's case, that was going to be easier said than done.

She'd not long set off when her mobile rang. Lorne put it on hands free and answered it. "Katy, is that you?"

"Hi, Lorne. Sorry. Had problems getting hold of Roberts yesterday. I managed to pin him down today—not literally." They both laughed. "He has a few reservations, but on the whole, he's agreed to me helping you out occasionally."

Lorne thumped the air excitedly with one hand, while the other firmly held the steering wheel. "That's great. Dare I ask what his reservations were?"

Katy hesitated for a moment or two. "Actually, he was a bit narked that you hadn't contacted him directly and chose to go through me instead. I also got the impression that he was hoping you'd reconsider your retirement and come back to the team."

"Oh, dear. Maybe he has a point about contacting him personally. I'm afraid I let my excitement get the better of me there. As for coming back to the team, I'm not sure that was ever on the agenda.

Returning once was bad enough for me. Anyway, I've told Linda that I'll be taking on her case. Talking of which, there's been a significant development."

"Go on," Katy said, sounding intrigued.

"Well, I dropped a dog off at their place this evening—just on my way home now, as it happens. Anyway, it turns out that one of Linda's flatmates has also fallen victim to this Gibson bloke." Not confident with driving and holding a conversation Lorne pulled into the curb.

"What? You're kidding?"

"Nope. The police have told Linda that, as there was no DNA evidence, there's little they can to do about Gibson."

"What about the other girl? Did she report the incident when it happened?" Katy asked.

"No. She was too ashamed to. Didn't say a word to anyone, apparently. She's very timid. Was petrified of the dog at first. By the time I left, she was starting to make friends with him."

"She has to come in and see us now. You told her that, right?"

"I did. She'll be reporting the incident in the next few days. Again, without evidence, it's not going to go anywhere, and your lot might even think it's a fake account of what happened, once they learn she resides at the same address as Linda."

"I'll see what I can do my end. Chase up who went to see Gibson and what their take is on it and get back to you. Other than that, not sure what else we can do."

"Thanks, Katy. It's a start at least. I've left Blackie with the girls; he's a German shepherd. I think they'll feel more secure with him around. The one thing that's niggling me, though, is the fact that two of the three girls have been raped by this guy, and during Linda's attack, he threatened to rape the third girl, Linda's sister, Fiona. Which leads me to suspect he's somehow keeping tabs on them."

"That fits. In what way, do you think?"

Lorne thought about that for a few seconds as she watched the traffic whiz past her parked car. "Maybe he's stalking them. Keeping an eye on their flat. I don't know how, but I intend to find out."

Katy gave a brief laugh. "I'm sure you do. I'll do the necessary at this end and get back to you in a day or two with the information. Talk soon, Lorne."

"Thanks, Katy. You're a star."

Lorne hung up and pulled out into a convenient slot in the traffic. Two miles from home, she stopped at the local chip shop and ordered three portions of cod and chips with a side order of mushy peas for her father. The aroma of food filled the car by the time she arrived home fifteen minutes later.

While the three of them ate their meal out of the paper, Lorne relayed the devastating news that Ami had divulged when she'd dropped Blackie off.

"Jesus, no wonder the girls are so petrified," Tony said, placing his final chip in his mouth before he balled up the paper his food had been wrapped in and set it to one side.

"That's just it, love. Ami hadn't told the other girls before tonight."

"He's watching them." Tony ran his tongue over his lips, licking up the remaining salt from his dinner.

"That was my first thought, too. Although I didn't tell the girls that."

Her father nodded. "Very wise. No sense frightening the poor lasses any more than is necessary. Where do we go from here, Lorne?"

"First of all, I need to sort out a new car. The van's great for this business, but what with the name of the Rescue Centre plastered over the sides, it's going to be a bit of a give-away if I start following suspects in that."

Her father tutted and waved a hand in front of him. "Nonsense. What's mine is yours. Use the Nova until you get on your feet. If I'm running this place, I won't be able to go out gallivanting in it now, will I?"

"That's great, Dad, if you're sure. In that case, I'd like to get started first thing tomorrow." She popped the final piece of battered cod in her mouth and balled up her own paper, pausing mid-twist when she glanced sideways at the evening paper lying on the kitchen table, an image jumped out at her. "I don't believe it."

She handed the paper to Tony. "Well, what do you know. The bastard really does like the limelight, doesn't he?"

The picture was of Gibson, standing in the middle of a crowd of young city dealers, looking smug beyond words. The headline read: "New kid on the block blows his competitors out of the water."

Lorne felt her heart rate escalate as her gaze bored into that of the man staring back at her from the photo. "I think I'm going to enjoy bringing this 'New kid' down a peg or two."

CHAPTER TEN

The next day, Lorne shot out of bed with renewed vigour. Tony lifted his head off the pillow and glanced at the clock. Seeing it was only five thirty, he groaned and shoved his head under the pillow. Lorne sprang into action, impersonating a whirlwind on a mission. After gathering her clothes from the wardrobe and her underwear from the chest of drawers, she disappeared into the bathroom to shower.

Once fully clothed, she decided to let her hair dry naturally. Lorne leapt onto the bed beside her snoring husband and prodded him, "Hey, you. Time to get this show on the road."

Annoyed he hadn't stirred, Lorne shot her hand under the quilt. Tweaking a nipple, she repeated, "Time to get up, hon."

"Do I have to? Can't you do the chores in the morning? I promise I'll do them every evening," Tony's juvenile whining was muffled by the pillow still wrapped firmly around his head.

"Awww, sweetheart. You promised," she mimicked his whine and added an extra emphasis of her own.

Suddenly, the pillow hit her round the side of her head, and the quilt was thrown back over her. "Take the mickey out of me, would you? An MI6 agent who has killed people for doing less than you just did?"

Lorne laughed and threw the quilt back over him. "That's former MI6 agent, just in case you need reminding, Mr. PI. Now shift your well-rounded backside."

"You cheeky... Are you saying I've put on weight?" He took the artificial leg that was lying on the floor beside him, strapped it on, and jumped out of bed. Marching over to the full-length mirror, he dragged his hands down his stomach, which he'd pulled in so his ribs protruded slightly.

Lorne went up behind him and peered around his upper arm at his mirror image. "Now speak," she demanded, knowing that as soon as he let out a breath, his slight pot belly would promptly fall back into place.

He refused and marched into the bathroom.

Lorne placed a finger in her mouth and made a strike in the air. "My first win of the day, I think." She had a feeling she was going to enjoy working alongside her husband. Whether or not he'd feel the same after a few months—that remained to be seen.

She started the morning chores.

She was in the middle of exercising the dogs when her father joined her. "Hey, Dad. You're up early, couldn't you sleep?"

He pecked her on the cheek and ruffled the head of the setter dog that had come up to greet him. "I've had enough sleep, love. Just thought I'd lend a hand so that you could get on the road early."

"Dad, you're going to be working hard enough around here as it is. I'm sorry to dump all this on you." She placed an arm around his shoulders and hugged him tightly.

Her father hooked an arm around her waist in return. "I've been thinking."

Lorne frowned as she searched his face for a possible clue as to what he was going to say next. She saw none. "About what, Dad?"

His hand swept out in front of them. "This place. How to make it profitable."

Lorne unhooked his arm from her waist and turned to face him. "Not sure I'm going to like this, but go on."

"Why don't we expand? Make it a boarding kennel, too."

"What? You do remember I'm in the midst of starting up another business, don't you? Lord knows when I'll get the time to put more hours into this place." She ran an anxious hand over her face.

"That's the thing; you won't have to. What are we? Half an hour from the airport? That makes it an ideal location for boarding dogs while people jet off for their holidays. They could even drop the dogs off en route."

Lorne eyed her father with scepticism. One minute, he was tearing into her for expecting him to run the place while she carried out her PI duties, and the next, he was having some bizarre talk of expanding the business. "Crikey, Dad, this has come out of the blue."

"I know. I'm trying to think of the future. If you're expecting Charlie to take over the running of this place in a few years, I think you'll need to make the proposition more exciting for her. What does she have to look forward to at the moment, except cleaning up dog poop, feeding and exercising the dogs? This way, she'll have to deal with the general public, run the business—as in, take money for a service. Deal with potential customers over the phone. Personally, I think it will be the making of her." His enthusiasm and the pride he felt for his granddaughter was apparent by the twinkling in his hazel eyes.

Lorne chuckled. "You've really put some thought into this, haven't you? In such a short space of time. Let me think about it over the next few days, and then we'll both sit down with Charlie and put the plan to her at the weekend. In the meantime, why don't you make some calls? Try to find out what licences we'll need to obtain."

"Sounds good to me. Are you going to be long here?" her father asked, already setting off for the gate that led out of the compound.

"Another half an hour or so, why?"

"I'm making pancakes for breakfast. Thought I'd give my girl a treat on her first day back at work in the real world."

At the mention of pancakes, Lorne's stomach grumbled. "Sounds great, Dad. Lashings of apricot jam for me, please."

After her father left, she took the setter inside and placed it in a kennel with fresh water and a bowl of food. The dog attacked the food as if it would disappear into thin air at any moment if he didn't.

That was the trouble with strays. They tended to bolt their food down, remembering what it was like to go without for days on end.

"Hungry boy." Tony's voice startled her.

"I hope he finds a home soon. He's crying out to be loved by a kind family. I must remember to place an ad in the local over the weekend. John said he'd run one every week for free, providing he has the space in the column. It'd be daft not to take him up on his kind offer. Do you want to give me a hand?"

Lorne continued to exercise the dogs one by one, while Tony cleaned the kennels and replenished the water and food bowls.

Twenty minutes later, they walked through the back door of the house to the wonderful smell of freshly made pancakes. Lorne eagerly eyed the pile sitting on top of the range. Tony and she scrubbed their hands then tucked into the pancakes, the pile decreased rapidly one by one.

"Yum! You still make the best pancakes in Kent, Dad." Lorne wiped the side of her mouth where the apricot jam had oozed out of the pancake.

Her father joined them at the table. "Flattery will get you everywhere, love."

Tony nodded and swallowed his mouthful. "I can vouch for that, Sam, I've never tasted pancakes as good as these." He turned to Lorne. "What's up first, this morning?"

"I need to do an ad for the English setter. Dad, if I leave you the number for John, will you phone it through for me?"

"Of course. I'll be making a few calls today, as we discussed. One more won't make a difference."

"What's this?" Tony asked.

"I'll tell you in the car. I want to start making discreet enquiries about Gibson. We need to go to the club, but I don't think there will be anyone there until this afternoon. Maybe we'll head into the city first thing and see if we can find Gibson. Until I find out some gossip about him, it'll just be a case of surveillance to begin with, and I'd like to see if I can track down the ex-girlfriend later." Lorne popped another forkful of pancake into her mouth.

Tony nodded thoughtfully. "Makes sense to keep the guy under observation for a few days. Are you going to ring the girls to see how Blackie has settled in?"

"Thought I'd do that about lunchtime. Eat up, and we'll set off before the traffic starts to build up."

The traffic heading into London wasn't just bad—it was absolutely nightmarish. After paying the congestion charge, Lorne and Tony made their way into the heart of the money sector. At two minutes to seven thirty, she parked her father's car in a space close to Gibson's place of work and waited.

Tony looked at his watch. "I doubt he'll turn up until five minutes to nine."

He leaned his head against the headrest, and Lorne got the feeling he was about to sneak a quick forty winks. "We'll see. You could always make yourself useful and try to find us a coffee."

He reluctantly opened the car door and walked up the high street. Her wait was uneventful. He returned with two disposable coffee cartons and handed her one.

She took a sip and immediately screwed up her face. "Yuck! That's black and very strong."

"The guy said he was out of milk."

Lorne got out of the car and threw the carton in a nearby rubbish bin. When she returned to the car, she pointed out the side window towards the office block they were keeping an eye on. "That's him."

"Dressed to impress, I see." Tony retrieved his binoculars from the back seat.

Lorne nodded and watched as Gibson, walking with three young women who seemed to be hanging on his every word, laughed as they made their way towards the building. "Well, he doesn't seem to have a problem attracting the ladies, does he?"

Tony's expression was full of disgust. "If that's the case, then why does he have to go out and rape women?"

"That, dear hubby, is what I intend to find out. Maybe we'll get a better idea about what makes him tick this afternoon, when we try to track down his ex."

"Where to now?" Tony asked as the group they had been watching disappeared through the front door of the building and out of sight.

It was too early to go to the nightclub. Lorne mulled over her husband's question for several seconds. "I know. We've got a few hours to kill. Why don't we track down a printer and get some cards made?"

"Cards? As in business cards? For the PI business or the kennels?"

Lorne smiled at him and started the car. "Both, I suppose. Although I think we should concentrate on the PI business first, until Dad finds out if we can take in boarders or not."

The driver of a red sports car motioned for her to pull out in front of him, into a gap in traffic. Lorne acknowledged him with a quick wave and headed into town.

She parked on the third level of the multi-storey car park, and they took the stairs down to the shopping precinct.

"Here you go. I don't really think we should be spending out a fortune on top-quality printing yet, just in case," Tony noted as they stopped outside Kall Kwik, the printers.

Lorne raised a sceptical eyebrow. "And why's that, sweetheart?"

He smiled sheepishly and shrugged. "Just in case, you know."

She tutted and walked into the shop before him, not bothering to hold the door open. She heard him swear under his breath when the glass edge of the door connected with his forehead. Take that, big guy, for doubting me and my new business.

A young man in his late teens with a bad case of acne approached them. "Can I help you?"

Lorne looked around at all the equipment in the shop and at how many of the assistants were busy working, churning out printed letterheads or photocopying coloured flyers. "We'd like some business cards."

"Certainly. If you'd like to follow me." He walked through the shop to a table at the rear, which had several bulky sample books spread across its surface. "These are the cards that are outsourced, as we call it—a better quality product that our printers make off-site. The delivery is seven to ten days on those. Or we could quickly create you something on the computer and have them printed up on card within an hour or so."

"Sold. The latter option is fine by me. I—sorry, we—really need them today."

"No problem." The assistant left them and walked behind the expansive counter. He returned a few seconds, later carrying a laptop. "I'll just pull up the templates."

Lorne stared at the screen, agog at the hundreds of choices available. "Crikey, I wouldn't know what to choose. There is such a thing as too much choice, you know."

Tony gently moved Lorne to one side. "Right. We want plain white cards, nothing fancy. This font, Times New Roman. This size for the heading, and this one for the rest." Tony then wrote down the details the printers needed for the card and handed it to the young man. He glanced sideways at Lorne and winked at her.

She felt glad and relieved that she'd brought him along. She had a feeling the whole process would have taken her hours not minutes to sort out, otherwise. She nodded at the assistant. "That's what we want."

Amused, the assistant tapped away at the keyboard for the next five minutes, then swivelled the laptop in their direction.

When Lorne read the card, pride overwhelmed her, and her eyes unexpectedly misted up.

Tony flung an arm around her shoulders. "I take it you're happy with that?"

The words stuck in her throat and refused to pass her lips, she simply nodded her approval.

"Perfect. We'll be back in an hour or so," Tony told the assistant. "Come on, Mrs. Warner. We'll grab a coffee while we wait."

CHAPTER ELEVEN

An hour later, armed with their newly printed batch of business cards, Lorne and Tony headed through the city back out to where the nightclub was situated.

"How are we going to handle this?" Tony asked. She saw him cringe out of the corner of her eye as she grated her way through the gears after pulling away from the lights.

"Nicely, at first. I'm going to be up front with them. Tell them that we're PIs investigating an attack on their premises. Let's see what type of reaction we get. I'm sure the police have already questioned the manager about the incident; I'd be very surprised if they haven't."

"Did Katy say they had?"

Lorne looked at him. "I forgot to ask, to be honest. We'll soon find out, anyway."

They parked in the club's large car park at the rear and knocked on the back door. Lorne glanced at her watch; it was almost eleven. No response.

Tony banged his fist on the door and placed his ear against it. "Well, someone's in there; I can hear music."

"Shall we try round the front?" Lorne asked, looking over her shoulder.

When they arrived, they couldn't find any sign of a bell beside the big leatherette cushioned door, so Tony banged on it hard with his clenched fist, but it proved to be pointless.

Just when they were about to give up, a young woman walked up behind them. The blonde, in her twenties, was dressed in tight jeans and a low-cut red top.

She gave them a puzzled look and abruptly asked, "You want something?"

"To get in would be nice," Lorne replied with a smile. It was hard for Lorne to judge the way the blonde was appraising her; disdain came to mind.

"Why?" The girl's gaze turned to Tony. She looked him up and down with the same disapproving look.

Lorne smiled sweetly. "I'll tell the manager that, if you don't mind."

The blonde hitched up one of her shoulders. "He ain't in."

If you want to play games with me, sweetie, you're gonna have to do better than that. "And you'd know that how?"

"Sorry?"

"I just wondered if you had some kind of magic powers that allowed you to see through, what, a six-inch door?"

The girl gave her a disapproving glare. "I just know. He don't tend to arrive until middayish."

Lorne glanced at the clock on the church tower up the road, it was twenty minutes before midday. "Is that so? We'll come in and wait then, if it's all right with you."

The door swung open, and a scrawny guy with a short goatee beard cautiously eyed Lorne and Tony. "Mindy, good to see you. Come in, babe. And who are you?"

Tony took a step forward, but Lorne latched onto his forearm to stop him. She withdrew a newly printed card from her bag and handed it to the guy. "We're private investigators. We'd like to speak to the manager or owner of the club."

Mindy walked through the door and whispered something in goatee beard's ear.

He attempted to shut the door on them, but Tony was quicker. Yanking the door out of the guy's hand, Tony ushered Lorne before him and into the club. He stood a few inches in front of the man, resorting back to his MI6 intimidation tactics. "Thanks for the invite, pal."

The guy received the message and instantly backed down. "Go through to the bar. I'll give the boss a call."

Tony and Lorne waited, both sipping a glass of orange juice, on one of the violet velour banquettes in the main bar area. The nightclub looked as though it had recently been refurbished.

Lorne admired the designer's expertise in creating a sumptuous atmosphere. The blend of violet, chrome, and glass had given the club a truly decadent feel. She'd need to come back at night with all the disco lights working, just to see if the designer had pulled off the desired effect he or she had tried to accomplish.

After twenty minutes, Tony's patience ran out of steam. He drummed his fingers on the glossy black table. "What the hell is taking him so long?"

"Not a strong suit of yours, is it?" Lorne said amused.

"What, patience? Not really. Guess I tend to think people are pulling a fast one when they delay meetings."

Lorne shook her head and glanced at Mindy behind the bar. "Trouble is, we don't know where he lives, Tony. His house could be out in the sticks, somewhere fifty miles away. Or he could've been in a meeting or something. I'm going to ask the charming Mindy a few questions while we wait."

"Huh! Best of luck with that."

The girl saw Lorne approach and busied herself with cleaning the already sparkling bar. Lorne perched on a stool in front of her. "Been working here long, have you?"

"A year or so," Mindy replied tersely.

Lorne nodded and played with a coaster. "So you know quite a few of the regulars then?"

"Kind of." The colour rose in Mindy's cheeks.

Hmm... My guess is she knows a few of the regulars more than a little bit. "Do you have a boyfriend, Mindy?"

The girl's expression turned to one of confusion. "What's that got to do with you?"

"Doesn't it go with the territory? You must get chatted up all the time, don't you?"

The girl shook her head as she wiped the bar faster. "Yeah, like on a daily basis. It gets tedious after a while. Still not sure where you're heading with your questions." She paused and carefully studied Lorne.

"Have you had any dealings with a Graham Gibson?"

The girl's eyes went wide, and she began rubbing at the bar again, faster and harder, as she shook her head in denial.

Lorne placed her hand on top of Mindy's. "Something tells me that you have. Come on, Mindy. What do you know?"

The other woman's eyes moistened, and she nervously looked around the club. "I can't say."

Lorne lowered her voice and leaned towards her. "Why?"

She backed away from the bar and scraped a nervous hand through her hair. "Please, I just can't. I've said too much already."

"But you haven't told me anything, yet. Has he hurt you, Mindy?"

Before the woman could answer, a thickset man appeared beside Lorne. Mindy left the bar, her head bowed as if ashamed.

"And you are?" The man eyed Lorne with disdain.

"Lorne Simpkins. You?" She offered her hand, but he ignored it. Sensing trouble, Lorne motioned with her head in Tony's direction. "And he's my partner."

Slowly the man turned to face Tony, whose mouth stretched into a menacing grin.

A half-smile replaced the man's sneer. He offered his hand.

Lorne shook the offered hand, regretting it when he gave an intimidating squeeze that made her wince.

"Ted Owen. I own this place. The doorman said you're a PI?"

"That's right. I—sorry, we—wanted to ask you a few questions about an incident that took place last week outside your club."

Owen dropped on to the stool next to Lorne. "The incident that the police have already asked me about, you mean?"

"Probably. The rape incident."

He shrugged. "I can only tell you what I told the boys in blue. Afraid I know nothing about it."

Lorne had expected that response. She kept her voice calm, despite the frustration building in the pit of her stomach. "What about CCTV. You do have that, don't you?"

"Of course." His tone had turned cocky, and his eyes were smiling. "Unfortunately, we had a glitch in the system that evening."

Lorne raised an eyebrow. "A glitch? Or did someone turn the machine off?"

Owen laughed and looked over at Tony. "Your partner here has a vivid imagination." His gaze returned to Lorne. "It was a definite glitch. Now, if you don't mind, I have a few calls to make." He got off the stool and thrust out his hand again for her to shake.

Lorne decided to push him further. "I'm guessing one of those calls is going to be to Graham Gibson."

For a fraction of a second, he glared at her before his half-smile returned. "And why would I do that?"

"You're not denying that you know him, then?"

"He's a regular punter. Why would I deny that?"

Lorne slipped off her stool and took a step toward him. "I don't know. Maybe covering up for a friend of yours—though why anyone would want to be friends with a scumbag like that is beyond me."

His brow furrowed. "Scumbag? You have one bitch's word that he did it. You do know he's well off, don't you?"

Lorne laughed. "You know what, Mr. Owen? Sometimes his type are the worst. Often they think just because they're wealthy, they can have anything that takes their fancy—by force, if necessary."

"Says you."

"Says me and ten years' experience in the Met, dealing day in and day out with the likes of him. Criminals come in all shapes and sizes, and from every conceivable background, Mr. Owen. None of them have it engraved on their foreheads—although if I had my way, I'd ensure they did. I'll let you get on with making your calls, and if you should happen to ring Mr. Gibson, be sure to let him know I'm on his case, won't you?"

Owen smirked. "I'll be sure to do that."

Lorne and Tony left the club.

Outside, she told Tony, "I hate it when they throw the 'you know he's rich, don't you' card around. If I wasn't determined before to nail Gibson, I bloody well am now."

CHAPTER TWELVE

Fiona arrived home from work to find Ami staring at Blackie. The dog was busy chomping his way through a rawhide bone that Lorne had left for him. "Everything all right?"

The poor girl almost jumped out of her skin at the sound of Fiona's voice. "Er... Sorry. I was miles away."

"Are you okay?" Fiona placed her handbag on the coffee table and sat on the sofa next to her flatmate. Blackie stirred long enough to wag his tail at Fiona before he returned to chewing on his bone.

Ami's gaze remained on the dog. "Just thinking," she replied sadly.

Fiona placed a tentative arm around her shoulder. "About anything in particular, hon?"

Ami expelled a large breath. "I should've told my parents. You know, about the assault. My mum is going to be devastated when she finds out."

Fiona had been thinking the same thing all day, with regard to telling her own parents about Linda, and had yet come to the conclusion whether it would be the right thing to do or not. Their father had recently suffered a mild heart attack and was under strict instructions from the doctor to avoid stressful situations. The jury was still out on if she should confide in her mother, knowing that her father always intuitively sensed when something was troubling his wife.

"I agree it's difficult. Linda and I are in the same position. I take it you went to the police station today to file the complaint?"

"I did. They told me, as the incident happened a few weeks ago, they were doubtful about any positive outcome."

Fiona withdrew her arm and clasped her hands tightly together in her lap. "Lorne warned us that might happen. I'll give her a ring later; see what she suggests. Thanks for going down there, Ami. You never know. It might make a difference someday. Is Linda in her room?"

"She wasn't feeling too well. She went to lie down a few hours ago when I got in from uni. I took Blackie for a walk in the park so Linda could have some peace and quiet. I didn't know whether to check on her or not."

"Thanks. I take it you and Blackie are getting along okay? Not sure about you, but I feel a darn sight safer knowing he's around." Fiona stood up.

Ami shrugged. "I suppose so. He seems settled here. Any idea what you want for dinner? I thought I might make a beef and ginger stir fry. Do you think Linda would like that?"

Fiona smiled and moved over to Linda's door. "She loves your stir fries. Go ahead and start. I'll check how she is and then come help chop the veggies."

She pushed open the bedroom door. The room was dark, apart from the dim ray of light showing at the edge of the curtain. "Linda? Are you awake?"

A small moan told her yes. Fiona gently sat down on the bed beside her sister. She smoothed back a lock of hair that had flopped across Linda's face. "How's your head?"

Linda gingerly sat up and switched on the lamp beside her. Blinking against the sudden brightness, she replied, "Like it belongs to someone else."

"Can I get you some tablets?"

"I took some a couple of hours ago. You know I can't stand taking tablets unnecessarily. You don't think he did any permanent damage, do you?"

Fiona shook her head. "I wouldn't have thought so, sweetie. Maybe it's more about you not sleeping well. That can take a toll on you. I hear you tossing and turning all night long. I'm wondering if you should see a doctor."

"A shrink? That kind of doctor?" Linda shrieked.

"All right, calm down. It was just a suggestion."

"The only thing that will give me peace at night is the thought of that pervert being locked up or at least off the streets. He taunts me, fills my dreams every night. Every hour of the day, I can still smell his vile breath and feel his hands touching me, groping me. It's a horrible feeling, Fi, and I just want it to stop."

"I'm sorry. I feel so helpless. I wish I could do more for you. I thought getting a dog would help set your mind at ease, but that doesn't seem to be the case. I know it's easier said than done, but you have to try to move on. If you don't, it's as though he's continually destroying your life. I don't want him to do that."

Tears welled in Linda's already puffy eyes. "If only we could do something. The police are hopeless—without any evidence, that is. It galls me to think he's out there. For all we know, he could be lining up his next victim."

"Don't say that, Linda."

"It's true. I've been thinking. I've got little else to do, right? What are the odds on both Ami and I being raped by the same person? Do you think he's stalking us? Keeping an eye on the place? How did he know I had a sister? I didn't tell him, and you've never been to the club with me, so how would he know?"

Fiona let her sister's words sink in for a minute or two, her sister had a valid point. "Let's see what Lorne digs up on this bastard and go from there."

Linda frowned. "What do you mean? I know that look. You have a plan festering, don't you?"

Fiona placed a hand to her chest. "Who, me?"

"Yes, you. Come on. Let me in on it. I hope you're not going to do anything stupid, Fi. The guy is not worth getting into trouble for."

"Let my plan fester a little while longer, and then I'll let you in on it. Ami's cooking one of your favourites. Are you up to eating anything?"

Linda swung her legs off the bed and slipped on her towelling robe. "Maybe if I had something to eat, it would ease my headache."

"That's the spirit. Umm... Would you mind if I popped out this evening?"

"Why should I? I've come to a few decisions today. This guy isn't going to stop me living my life the way I want to live it: free of fear. I'm going back to work in the next few days. We all should go on with our lives as normal. You go out. Ami and I will be okay with Blackie here to watch over us."

Fiona released the breath she had been holding in. Gone was Linda's flinching when someone spoke. Fiona could see a determination that she knew would go a long way in assisting her sister to recover from her ordeal.

The two sisters linked arms and went in search of Ami in the kitchen. The wonderful aroma of their flatmate's skill brought a smile to Fiona's face. Even Blackie was standing at the kitchen doorway, eagerly wagging his tail.

After eating her meal, Fiona changed into a pair of jeans and her new blouse. She left the bedroom just as the front door bell rang. "That'll be Jason. Don't wait up." She gave Linda a quick peck on the cheek and opened the door.

All through the evening, Jason twittered on about what he'd been up to since their last date. Fiona let him. Her mind was elsewhere, anyway.

She felt his hand cover hers.

"Fi? Have you heard a word I've been saying this evening?"

They had been going out with each other, on and off, for five years, and she had always found him interesting. Jason was a gentle, considerate man who lived life to the fullest extent.

"I'm sorry, Jason."

Before she could say anything else, he leaned over the table and silenced her with a gentle kiss. "No need to apologise, love. How is Linda? I wasn't sure whether you'd want to talk about her or not this evening."

"She's getting there. Before dinner, she told me she was thinking about going back to work. That's a good sign, isn't it?" She took a sip of wine and then ran her finger around the rim.

"Too right it is. I'm sorry for not being able to help more. I feel so inadequate. No news on the police front, is there?"

"No. Actually, there's something I haven't told you."

Jason took a drink from his own glass. "What's that?"

"It's come to light that Ami was raped last month by the same guy."

He bounced back in his chair as if he'd been hit by a thunderbolt. "What?" Then he sat forward again and grasped her hand tightly in both of his. "But why didn't she tell you?"

Fiona shrugged. "She was too ashamed. She hasn't even told her mum yet."

"Ami reported it to the police at the time, didn't she?"

"Unfortunately not. She went down the station yesterday, but they sounded pessimistic about their chances of nailing the bastard. They're going to question him about both incidents, but they don't hold out much hope of making anything stick. No evidence.""That's terrible. So what happens now?"

Fiona mulled over his question for a while. "I've employed the services of a PI. She's an ex-Met detective. We'll see what she can come up with. You met her the other night."

"The woman you got Blackie from?"

She nodded. "Yep. At least the dog has given us some peace of mind. After his threat—"

Jason's eyes widened. Fiona cringed.

"Whoa, hold on a minute. What threat? You mean this guy has been in touch since?"

Fiona swallowed. "Not exactly. The night Linda was, er... raped, he told her that if she fought him or screamed that he would come after me."

"You're kidding me?" His mouth dropped open.

"Sorry, hon. I shouldn't have told you. That's why we got Blackie. I'm safe. Please don't worry. I go to work and come straight home every day. This is the first time I've ventured out since it happened. I just wish there was something we could do to stop this guy from raping anyone else."

Thoughtful silence settled between them.

Jason's clenched fist connected with the table, making Fiona jump. "There is," he said, an evil smile curling his lip.

"What?"

"We go after him. Vigilante-style, if necessary."

Fiona was shocked by his statement but it caused an idea she'd hatched a few days earlier to run through her mind.

CHAPTER THIRTEEN

Saturday morning arrived with the sound of Charlie bouncing excitedly through the back door. Lorne glanced at her watch; it was a little before eight.

She couldn't help but wonder how long her daughter's enthusiasm for mucking out the kennels and other chores was going to last. She would tackle Charlie about the proposition she had for her after they took care of the necessary chores.

The menial labour was a welcome relief to get away from the computer for a while. The day before, Lorne had spent over ten hours researching Gibson. The research had thrown up some surprising results. She'd established that he came from not only a rich family, but a very rich family—the kind of family who sent their kids to the best public school money could buy: Eton. He'd achieved several accolades for his sporting abilities, as captain of both the rugby team and the rowing team too.

The question still haunted her. So why had someone from such a privileged background turned out to be a rapist?

The morning flew past. During lunch Lorne, Charlie, Tony and her father sat down for a serious discussion.

Lorne broached the subject of running the kennels. "So, Charlie, we've been chatting, and we want to run something past you."

Charlie placed her mug on the table. "Sounds ominous. Have I done something wrong?"

The three adults around the table all laughed, and the worry lines disappeared from Charlie's forehead.

"On the contrary. Actually, we are very impressed with the way you've adapted to helping out around here. We'd like to put a proposition to you."

Charlie tilted her head, looking intrigued. "Go on."

"I know we've spoken a little about your future, and the last time we spoke, you weren't exactly sure what career path you wanted to take. Has that changed at all?"

"Not really, Mum. I still have a tiny part of me that wants to join the police, but then I've seen how the force treat their women officers, and it's made me want to reassess that decision. Why? What did you have in mind?"

Lorne spread her arm out to the side. "This place."

"I don't understand. You and Tony run this place."

"Well... For the time being, and with Tony's and my help, your grandfather is going to be running the place. We were hoping that you could take over once you leave school. If you wanted to, that is?"

Charlie's face lit up as if a thousand bulbs were planted under her epidermis. "Really? You mean it? But what are you and Tony going to do?"

Lorne placed her hand on Tony's. "We're going to become private investigators."

"Holy crap! Er... sorry. That's brilliant. My God, this is the best news I've heard in ages. We could all do it. Be private eyes I mean." She clapped her hands together.

Lorne struggled to keep a straight face. "Umm... First things first, young lady. It takes experience to be a PI—"

"Mum, give me a break. I know that. I'm not saying any time soon. But maybe in a few years?"

"We'll see. Now, getting back to our little plan. Your grandfather has been making some enquiries about turning this place into a boarding kennel to run alongside the rescue centre."

Charlie nodded. "Makes sense. It might encourage people to take one of the rescue boarders home with them when they come and pick their own dogs up."

Lorne couldn't help but be impressed with her daughter's thinking. She really had matured over the last few months. "That's what we thought. We still have a little research to do on that side of things, but initial enquiries have come up with positive results so far. It would mean you having to deal with the general public, though. Are you up to that?"

"If you'd asked me that question last year, I would have said no way. However, the counsellor has told me I've come a long way in the last few months. So much so, in fact, that she thinks the sessions can come to an end soon."

Lorne stood up, wrapped her arms around her daughter, and squeezed tight. The knowledge that the Unicorn's hold over her daughter would soon come to an end was the best news she'd had in a very long time. "Darling, that's wonderful news. This calls for a celebration. We're all going out to a fancy restaurant tonight, on me."

"Mum, get off me. I told you I'd get over it, didn't I? I have your stubborn genes, don't forget."

"Be right back." Lorne heard her father and Tony congratulating Charlie as she made her way into the lounge to find the phone. Before she could ring the restaurant, the phone rang in her hand. She answered, "Hello?"

Silence.

"Hello?" she asked again, more loudly.

A muffled voice replied, "Leave well alone, bitch!" Then the caller hung up.

Lorne was staring at the phone when Tony came in.

He asked, "Who was that?"

"Not sure. Although I can hazard a guess."

He raised a quizzical eyebrow. "What did the caller say, Lorne?"

"He told me to back off, in no uncertain terms. He's got two hopes of that happening—Bob Hope and no bloody hope. Cheeky bastard. Let's see if his number shows up." Lorne redialled the number and wasn't surprised when it rang and rang. "Probably a call box somewhere, the gutless piece of shit."

"Let's not let it spoil the weekend. We'll pay the guy a visit on Monday—how's that? At work, if you like. That should knock the crap out of him."

Lorne smiled. She liked the way her husband was thinking. "Agreed. Maybe it's time we tightened the screws a little. I'm going to give Fiona a ring, see how things are with the girls."

Tony kissed her cheek lightly and walked back out into the kitchen.

"Hi, Fiona. I'm sorry, did I wake you?"

Fiona coughed. "Lazy Saturday lie-in after a hectic week. I was just getting up, is that you, Lorne?"

"It is. How's the boy settling in?" Lorne sat down on the sofa and booted her laptop to check her email.

"He's doing great. We're all spoiling him rotten. He's grown very attached to Ami. Hang on a sec—yep, I can't see either of them here; she must have taken him out for his walk. The last few days, she's been up with the birds to take him out. Who'd have thought it? Usually on a Saturday, she doesn't surface until mid-afternoon. Apparently, Blackie's brought her out of her shell."

"That's excellent news. And how's Linda, dare I ask?" Lorne tapped in her password as she spoke, and the email notification popped up that she had five new messages. She scrolled through the first four and opened the final message, a replica of the message she had received in the phone call. She switched on the printer and printed a copy, intending to give it to Katy as proof of Gibson's harassment, although the email address looked suspiciously like one that had been made up specifically for the occasion. She'd been so engrossed in printing the email off that she'd forgotten that Fiona was talking to her.

"... Anyway, she seems to be getting stronger, physically and mentally. Any news at your end, Lorne?"

"Not so much at the moment. Tony and I called in at the nightclub to question the owner but drew a blank. He wasn't very cooperative, I'm afraid. We're intending to pay Gibson a visit at his work on Monday."

"Really? That's brave of you."

Lorne wasn't sure if she should tell Fiona about the threatening call and email she had received. She decided against it. "Brave or stupid—not sure which, Fiona. We'll see on Monday. You have a good weekend. Don't hesitate to get in touch, day or night, okay?"

"That's reassuring. Thanks, Lorne. Let me know what the scumbag says on Monday, will you?"

"Sure, no problem."

Lorne disconnected the call and stared down at the email she'd printed off and thought. Despicable piece of dirt. Well, when I've finished with you, matey, Mummy and Daddy won't be able to buy you out of trouble anymore.

* * *

Gibson watched the girls' flat from his hiding place, behind the parked transit van opposite.

The Chinese girl came into view around the corner. What's this? They've got a dog now? Hmm... Well that throws a different light on things.

She had been easy to manipulate—they all were. Bloody women. Only good for one thing and most of the time, they managed to screw that up. All of them, give you the eye, a blatant come-on and yet balk at the first sign of contact.

Well, I'll show them that I'm not the type to be messed with.

A smile curved his lips. So you think a damn dog is going to protect you, do you? I have every intention of having a piece of that other girl's arse. She's who I'm really after the stuck-up bitch who looks down her nose at any man who glances her way. I've only seen her once but...

Gibson watched Ami walk up the street and enter the flat.

He waited a few minutes before he moved from his position and ducked down the alley running alongside the flat. Through a tiny hole in the fence, he saw Ami let the German shepherd out into the garden.

The dumb dog was incapable of picking up his scent and warn the girls he was nearby. If you think that mangy mutt is going to stop me from having some fun, you've got another think coming, sweethearts.

Gibson turned and made his way back to the car, already hatching a plan of how he was going to get to Fiona. He had something special lined up for her. The other girls had got off light compared to what he had planned for the snotty bitch.

He dipped around the next corner and slid into his Ferrari, and let out an hysterical laugh. You're a demented bastard, at times.

He drove away at speed, the acceleration made his mind work faster. By the time he reached his destination, he'd deviously hatched a master plan and slotted all the intricate parts together.

CHAPTER FOURTEEN

"Hi, Katy. How are things?" Lorne stared at the print-out of the email on the table in front of her.

"I know you well enough to know when something's up, Lorne. I can hear it in your voice. Come on. Give?"

Had Lorne become that easy to read since her retirement, or was Katy just getting more astute with experience? "Okay, we paid the nightclub owner a visit, but that was a waste of time. I'm guessing you guys got the same response as we did. Then yesterday, I received a crank call and a dubious email."

"Interesting. Yeah, we got nothing out of the owner of the club. Tell me more about the call and email?"

"There actually wasn't much to them, but they both said pretty much the same thing; warned me and Tony to back off. I'm betting it was Gibson behind them, but I have no way of knowing. I wondered if forensics could look into the ISP for me. I know it's a lot to ask."

Lorne heard Katy take a sharp breath. "Not sure about that, Lorne. Funds are getting tighter every day. Forward me a copy, and I'll see what I can do, AJ might be able to help out there. What do you plan on doing next—with the investigation, I mean?"

She hesitated for a moment before admitting, "Well, we thought we'd go pay our friendly rapist a personal visit."

"Shit! A word of warning, if I may. Be careful; his parents are well connected. If I were you I wouldn't go near him yet."

"Ah, but you're not me, and my hubby is an ex-MI6 agent. I think I have all the bases covered, don't you?"

Katy blew out an exasperated breath and snorted. "Just be careful. I've got to go. My gym instructor will be yanking on her ponytail wondering where I am. I'll be in touch soon. Take care."

"Have fun. I'll keep you up-to-date with what happens."

After hanging up, Lorne went back to her family in the kitchen and clapped to get their attention. "This is what I have planned for today: I'm making this a family fun day. It's been ages since we all spent the day together, what with getting this place up and running. I'm not saying that we take the day off—only that we make it a happy, special day, if you like. Tony, is the field at the back all fenced now?"

He nodded and tilted his head. "It is. Why?"

"I thought we'd give the dogs a good old run-around. They spend too much time cooped up in their kennels. The four of us can keep a proper eye on them. It'll do us all good to get some exercise too."

Charlie scraped her chair back and was halfway to the back door before she replied, "Excellent. I'll get the dogs' leashes ready. Come on, guys. Get a move on."

Sam Collins grunted as he stood up. "I think I'm getting too old for this lark, Lorne."

"Nonsense, Dad. I bet you're fitter than me at the moment."

"I doubt that. I suppose I'll appreciate our meal out this evening more if I burn off a few calories. Just a few, mind."

She punched Tony's shoulder lightly and pulled her reluctant husband out of his chair. "You want a sixteen-year-old to show you up? Come on. It'll be fun."

And it was. The dogs ran and ran, played, and rolled each other savouring their long awaited freedom. Charlie was chased the length and breadth of the field, laughing and screeching like a teenager should.

At four o'clock, they locked the exhausted dogs back in their kennels, showered and changed, and set off for the restaurant. Lorne had chosen an award-winning Indian restaurant for their family meal together, and they feasted on the banquet menu for four. Lorne loved to sample all the dishes on the menu instead of sticking to one boring main meal.

After their overindulgence at the restaurant, Lorne drove home and they all collapsed into bed, exhausted and satisfied by their fun day together.

The following morning, the sound of the telephone ringing woke a bleary-eyed Lorne. She cleared her throat and answered the phone by her bed; the clock read seven thirty-two. "Hello? You better have a good reason to be ringing me at this hour on a Sunday morning," she told the caller, a little offhandedly.

"Oh, I do."

Katy's tone immediately grabbed Lorne's attention. She sat upright against the headboard. "Go on. I'm listening."

"We've got him."

Lorne excitedly gave Tony a swift kick. He groaned and hid his head under the pillow. She lifted the pillow and whispered. "They've got him."

"Got who?" Tony mumbled groggily.

Lorne ignored him and asked Katy, "How? Did he rape someone else?"

"Yep. At least, he tried to."

"You're joking! Poor girl. What happened?"

Anger emanated from Katy as she recounted the incident. "The bastard had the audacity to try and rape the girl outside the nightclub this time. The thing is, someone heard the girl scream. She tried to escape him and ran up the alley. He chased her. She was lucky; two guys heard her scream and bolted up the alley to find out what was going on. They apprehended him, made a citizen's arrest, and confined him in the alley until our boys arrived. The girl was taken to hospital, but thankfully, she only suffered superficial bruising."

"So has he been banged up?"

"At the moment, yes. But he's got his high-profile brief on his way in to see him. To be honest, I don't think we'll be able to hold him for more than a few hours. I think the lines to the 'super' are already glowing red."

"Thanks for keeping me up to date, Katy. I guess I'll knock my plan on the head to visit him."

"Any further developments, I'll let you know. Speak soon."

Lorne let out a relieved sigh as she replaced the phone in its docking station on the bedside cabinet, but she was only too aware how cases like that one turned out. Best not get too excited about the news.

Tony slung a lazy arm across her and pulled her back down under the covers for a snuggle.

"Five minutes, then I need to get up and see to the animals."

Tony growled near her ear. "You need to take care of this animal first."

* * *

Charlie was hard at work long before Lorne and Tony finally surfaced. Leaving the mucking out in her daughter's capable hands, Lorne sat on the sofa and rang Fiona. "Hi, Fiona? It's Lorne."

"Crumbs. If you're ringing this early on a Sunday something, must be up. What is it?" Apprehension lingered in Fiona's voice.

Lorne expelled a heavy breath. "Good news and bad."

"Okay, good news first then, please."

"Gibson has been arrested."

"But that's wonderful news. Why?"

"He tried to attack another girl and got caught in the act."

Fiona sighed. "Not so wonderful, then."

"Yeah, you could say that. The bad news is that he's employed a top solicitor, who's on his way to the station now to see him. In my experience, these things have a tendency not to go according to plan, at least from the victim's point of view."

"I see. In that case I'm not going to tell the other girls yet. I wouldn't want to get their hopes up, anyway."

"I agree. I'll let you know what happens, I just wanted to keep you up to date with things. Be in touch soon. Enjoy the rest of your weekend."

"You, too. Thanks for ringing."

Lorne ended the call and sat back, contemplating how to proceed with the case. She'd need to wait to see what the outcome was with Katy before anything else. Maybe this is the frustrating side of being a PI that I hadn't envisaged not being in the thick of it at the station.

It was well past lunchtime before Lorne received an answer to her problem. The phone rang, and she pounced on it before anyone else could. "What happened?"

"The bastard blamed it all on the girl. We'll have to see what the Crown Prosecution Service has to say about things. Our hands are tied until then."

"Damn. Thanks, Katy. You know what? I think we'll still go pay him a visit at work tomorrow. You know how I love to see worms squirm."

Katy laughed, and they both hung up.

CHAPTER FIFTEEN

Outside the office block where Gibson worked, Lorne and Tony got out of their vehicle and headed inside the building. The reception area seemed to stretch skywards for miles. Metal railings acted as steps to the eye as it was drawn upwards to the angled glass roof.

The pretty receptionist smiled broadly at them as they approached.

"We'd like to see Graham Gibson, if that's possible?" Lorne asked.

"May I ask what it's concerning?" the receptionist asked, her smile never faltering.

"It's personal," Lorne responded vaguely.

"I see. Unfortunately, our employees aren't allowed to have visits of a personal nature. Maybe you should try and contact him at home this evening."

Lorne leaned in close and whispered, "When I say personal, I mean it's a surprise visit." She tapped her nose. "He's won a prize. We're from the local paper." Lorne pointed at Tony who was sporting his camera around his neck.

"Oh, how wonderful. I'm sure we can bend the rules an eensy weensy bit, this time. Take the lift up to the tenth floor. The whole office is open-planned. I seem to recall his desk is somewhere in the centre of the room. The names are suspended from the ceiling; you'll be able to find him easily enough once you're there."

"You're very kind. Oh, one last thing: I'd appreciate it if you don't tell anyone up there that we're on our way. I'd love to get his colleagues' reactions on film. It'll look more authentic for the article if their responses are more natural."

The receptionist gleefully rubbed her hands together. "Excellent. My lips are sealed."

On the journey over to the glass lift Tony said, "You'll get pimples on your tongue for telling porkies."

She stuck the tip of her tongue out at him. "Any appeared yet?"

He laughed and shook his head. "It is going to get you in big trouble one of these days."

Tony was probably right, and she hoped that wouldn't turn out to be the case today—at least, not before she had a chance of having some fun at Gibson's expense.

Lorne and Tony took the lift to the tenth floor of the building in silence. When the doors slid open, they stepped out into a narrow corridor. The door they needed was immediately to their right.

Her pulse was racing, she paused to take a calming breath before Tony pushed open the door and stood back for her to enter the room before him.

The receptionist had told them to look up at the ceiling for where Gibson's desk was located, but upon entering the room, Lorne knew that would be pointless. Before them stood a crowd of people; at a rough count, she estimated there to be at least fifty to sixty suited young businessmen and women. In the middle of the group stood a smiling Gibson, his arms loosely draped around a petite blonde who looked as if she hadn't eaten a proper wholesome meal in months, and a busty brunette who wore a skirt a few inches larger than a belt.

Lorne tried hard not to show the revulsion flowing through her. By the welcoming committee, it was obvious that the receptionist had gone against her word and pre-warned Gibson, which rankled Lorne. She heard Tony mumble something but couldn't make out what it was.

She put her shoulders back and plastered a false smile on her face, she approached the group with Tony a step or two behind her. "Mr. Gibson, I presume."

"The one and only," he smugly replied, much to the crowd's delight.

As much as she wanted to rip into him, Lorne knew she would have to bide her time and play along with her act. "I've heard such a lot about you. Any chance we talk privately somewhere?"

Gibson tilted his head back and laughed loudly. "Anything you have to ask me, you can do it in front of my adoring fans."

Anger bubbled dangerously near the surface. He really was an arrogant little fucker, one that she was going to enjoy tearing to bits. "I wouldn't want to keep your workmates from their jobs."

"They can make up the time later, during lunch or after work. They're as excited about my success as I am." He turned his head first one way and then the other, kissing the cheek of the girl who was attached to each arm.

That action sent Lorne's anger monitor into the red zone. "My partner here would like to take some pictures as we speak, if that's okay with you?" Lorne turned to Tony and raised her eyes to the ceiling. He smiled and pointed his camera in Gibson's direction. In other words he was ready, willing, and certainly able to help take him down.

Gibson turned his head to the right slightly and lifted his chin. "Fire away. This is my best side. Wouldn't you agree, girls?"

The girls giggled inanely.

"I'd like to ask some general questions first."

His smile broadened, and with his gaze glued on the camera, he nodded.

"So what kind of hobbies do you have, Mr. Gibson?"

He raised an eyebrow. "Oh you know, I work hard and play even harder."

Again his band of merry followers chuckled. Lorne ground her teeth together. "Meaning what, exactly?" she asked, trying her darnedest to keep her tone light and interested.

"Well, a job like this means that we get to entertain corporate clients at top restaurants—"

"Wouldn't that be classed as work-related? I'm talking about your off-duty activities, things that occupy your spare time." Lorne shuffled closer to Gibson as the group began to dwindle. She didn't want the group to dissipate too much before she hit him where it hurt.

"Oh, I see. I usually hang out in a nightclub in town. When I'm not there, I go to the gym around the corner."

Lorne nodded. "Can I ask what you did over the weekend? I mean, did you go there as usual this weekend?"

His smile slipped momentarily, but to Lorne's surprise, he cast a nervous eye over the gathering crowd and quickly reinstated it. "Hmm... Let me think," he said, keeping his adoring fans on tenterhooks.

Sensing this was the right time to challenge him she asked, "Think up a suitable lie, you mean?"

His brow furrowed. He let go of the two girls and took a step toward Lorne, possibly intending to intimidate. "Meaning?" he retorted, matching her sharp tone.

She stood her ground. "Why don't we tell your colleagues where you spent Saturday night, for instance?"

Lorne observed the crowd, who in turn were eyeing Gibson with more than a touch of interest.

He fidgeted with his tie, pulling the knot tight up under his chin. "Saturday, you say? Now, where was I?"

Lorne played along for a few seconds, then started making the sound of a police siren, just for fun. "Does that help?" she asked, innocently fluttering her lashes. Above the noise of the camera shutter, she heard Tony snort.

"Who the fuck are you, lady?" He looked as though his poise had been made of porcelain and someone had just tapped it, shattering it into a million tiny pieces.

"Ah, finally the penny has dropped, Mr. Gibson. I take it you aren't going to enlighten your colleagues about your activities on Saturday night, after all?"

Out of the corner of her eye, Lorne saw Tony lower the camera, his stance ready for a possible attack by Gibson.

"Get the fuck out of here. You have no right being here. Someone call security to get this pair of lowlifes out of here."

Lorne leaned in. "A name that would suit you more than us, I fear, Gibson. Either you tell them, or I will. Which do you prefer?" she asked in a hushed voice.

A snarl tugged at his mouth. "You wouldn't dare."

"A word of warning, Mr. Gibson: I always rise to a challenge."

He folded his arms and tapped his foot, challenging her further.

"Very well. As my friend here isn't willing to divulge his weekend activities to his workmates, I'll do it for him." The chattering of the crowd died down.

Once she had everyone's attention, Lorne asked, "Perhaps you'd like to share with your workmates what the food is like in a police cell?"

Gasps rippled through the crowd as expressions changed from joyfulness to shock.

Lorne gazed back at Gibson; his eyes were squeezed tightly shut. Seconds later, they flew open, and the rage was evident for all to see. "Bitch. I repeat: Who the fuck are you?"

Lorne smirked and handed him a business card. "I think you know who I am already, as your mate at the nightclub has probably already contacted you, but in case your memory is a tad rusty, here you go." For those surrounding them, she added, "I, Mr. Gibson, am your worst nightmare. Do you want to tell your colleagues the circumstances behind your unintentional stay at the nick?"

He crumpled the card and dropped it on the floor, then scraped one of his hands through his short hair. Lorne got the impression that, had his hair been longer, he would have tugged clumps of it out by its roots in frustration.

Before Gibson could answer, a voice boomed out across the office. "What the bloody hell is going on here? I've told you before, this ain't no kindergarten. Get on with your work."

The crowd scattered, albeit reluctantly, to reveal a steel-grey haired man in a crisp white shirt and pinstriped trousers. He walked towards them, frowning. "Gibson?"

Lorne heard the rapist gulp and watched the colour enflame his cheeks. "Er... Sorry, Mr. Johnson. These people were just leaving."

Lorne seized the opportunity to embarrass Gibson further. Holding out her hand, she approached Mr. Johnson. "I'm Lorne Simpkins. Sorry about this. We'll be out of your hair soon. I just need to ask Mr. Gibson here a few questions."

The man's confused gaze slipped between Lorne and Gibson. "Questions? Are you the police?"

"Ah, I used to be. Former detective inspector in the Met, actually. Now, I've gone private, you might say."

"I see, I think. And what, might I ask, do you want with Gibson here?" Gibson opened his mouth to speak, but Johnson stopped him with a hand motion. "I was asking the nice young lady, not you."

Nice young lady. Lorne chuckled inwardly. Well, she hadn't been called that in a while.

"Actually my partner and I wanted to know why Mr. Gibson here takes it upon himself to threaten young women." Lorne glanced around the room and saw several women's heads drop back to the work in front of them. Obviously, some of them had already had Gibson's unwanted attention heaped upon them. While a few of his colleagues fawned all over him, others clearly kept their distance.

"Threaten? In what respect?" Johnson snapped back.

"Apart from sending me threatening emails and making similar calls, my client has already been threatened." Lorne was careful not to mention the rapes because of the lack of evidence in Linda and Ami's cases.

"Is this true, Gibson?" Johnson's tone brokered no nonsense.

"I haven't... When?" Gibson blustered.

"Come now, Gibson. Do we really have to tell your boss where you spent Saturday night?"

Johnson looked at Lorne. "Tell me," he ordered bluntly.

"Can't we do this privately?" Gibson asked, surveying the office.

"I don't mind, either way. On second thoughts, you were eager to share your news with your colleagues before when you thought we were reporters. What's the problem now? Afraid they'll see you in a different light?"

"Here is just fine. Please tell me what Gibson has done." Johnson demanded impatiently.

Gibson collapsed into his chair, placed his elbows on the table, and buried his head in his hands as Lorne told his boss what he'd been up to.

"What?" Johnson shouted in disbelief. He scowled at his employee, who was purposefully avoiding any form of eye contact.

"It's true, I'm afraid," Lorne insisted.

Johnson was shaking his head in disgust when he asked Lorne, "You say the unfortunate victim is your client?"

"No, I've yet to speak to the victim. I've known about Gibson's penchant for threatening and attacking women for a few weeks, now. My client's sister and her friend were assaulted by him. Unfortunately, there was little evidence for the police to bring charges. Gibson is—or was—very clever in that he covered his tracks well. After his latest victim on Saturday night, though, the Crown Prosecution Service will now have to look at all three cases and any others that arise in the meantime. Once news of the case gets leaked to the local newspaper, it's not uncommon for other victims to get in touch with the police to state they have been attacked by him too." She told Johnson hoping that her words would scare the crap out of Gibson.

Gibson thrust his chair back with such force that it tipped over. He marched over to Lorne.

Tony stood in front of her and warned, "Back off, shit face."

"It's lies, all lies."

"And why would these women lie about a thing like that, Gibson?" Johnson asked, sounding perplexed.

"Envy, jealousy, call it what you will," Gibson retorted venomously.

Lorne admired the way Johnson was standing up to Gibson. Despite the family's reputation, the man obviously didn't care or worry about the consequences.

"That's bullshit. You know what? I've had it up to here with you. The last few months, you've screwed up that many accounts, and I've brushed them under the carpet. I'm sick to death of giving you one more second chance. Pack up your desk. As of now, you're suspended for the rest of the week, at least. I'll see how the board of directors view these charges and ring you on Friday," Johnson told him, then said to Lorne, "I appreciate you coming here today and informing us of this incident. This firm will not tolerate such abhorrent behaviour from its employees."

"Believe me when I say the pleasure was all mine, Mr. Johnson." Lorne smiled at the man and glanced over at Gibson, who was busy collecting his belongings, muttering expletives under his breath. "Our work is done. Oh, and if any of you ladies have had an altercation with Gibson in the past, I'll leave my card on the desk here. We'll be going now. Thanks for your time." She held up a card and placed it on the desk beside Johnson before turning back in the direction of the lift.

"Good riddance," Gibson called after them.

Lorne chuckled when she heard an irate Johnson tongue-lashing Gibson as they left.

"It's not been a good few days for Gibson, has it?" Tony said during the journey back down in the lift.

"Let's hope the next few months are hell for him. I just hope the girls will be strong enough to face him in court."

CHAPTER SIXTEEN

Six months later.

Lorne raced around before the sun rose up in the morning sky. This was the day Gibson would hopefully get his comeuppance.

There was a lot of work to do around the Rescue Centre before she could set off for the courthouse. Although her father had said that he would see to the day to day running of the centre, the past few weeks, he'd struggled to stay on top of the daily chores. She should never have put the onus on him at his age. She'd taken some well-deserved flak from her sister, Jade, for putting their father under too much stress.

Lorne ran across the courtyard and back into the house. "Come on, Tony! What's keeping you?" Lorne called up the stairs.

A disgruntled Tony slowly made his way down the stairs. His face was pale, and beads of sweat glistened on his forehead. "I'll do what I can, love, but I'm not feeling a hundred percent."

He reached the bottom step.

She felt his cheek and forehead, turned him around, and patted his bottom. "Go on back to bed. Let me go finish with the animals, and then I'll come and tend to you and Dad. Looks like you've got the same bug Dad picked up."

"Well, if you're sure. I'll see you later," Tony croaked.

Lorne forced herself up a gear. By seven thirty, she had all the dogs fed and watered. The kennels could be cleaned later, after she returned from her day in court.

At eight o'clock, she rustled up some cereal and toast and took them in to her father. His ashen face creased in pain as he sat up in bed. Lorne placed the cushioned tray in front of him and refilled the water glass by his bed. "Feeling any better, Dad?"

"Worst bug I've ever had. It has drained me of all my energy. I'm sorry to let you down, love. I know you were relying on me, especially with what's going on today. Tony's lending a hand though, right?"

Lorne shook her head. "No worries, Dad. Everything's in hand. Tony seems to have come down with the same bug. He looks awful as well. I sent him back to bed. Look, eat what you can to try to keep your strength up. I'll take Tony up his breakfast and call back to get your tray in a little while. Do you need anything else?"

"Not for now. Thanks, love. Sorry I'm so useless at the moment."

She pecked her father's cheek. "Nonsense, Dad. I'm sorry I lumbered you with this place at your time of life when you should be taking things easy. See you in a few minutes."

Lorne left her father and rushed through to the kitchen to prepare Tony's breakfast, but the ringing telephone interrupted her.

She didn't hesitate to answer it; there hadn't been any threatening calls since they'd visited Gibson at his place of work. "Hello?"

"Hi, Lorne. It's Katy. All set for the big day, are you?"

Lorne carried the phone through to the kitchen and continued to prepare Tony's breakfast. "Just about, Katy. There are no last-minute hiccups on your end, are there?"

"Stop worrying, everything will turn out fine. We have him by the short and curlies on this one. I've never been more confident about a case."

Lorne laughed. "Oh, yeah. I forgot how experienced you are. You've had hundreds of cases go to trial, haven't you?"

"Smart arse! You know what I mean. DCI Roberts is confident that this will have a positive outcome. I wanted to check in to see what time you'll be at the courthouse."

"At the moment, I'm running behind schedule. Both Tony and Dad are ill in bed. You know how it is. Something always comes up to wreck well-laid plans. I'm just going to take Tony his breakfast up before I jump in the shower." She glanced up at the clock on the wall above the back door. "Shit, it's almost quarter past. I better get a move on."

"You go. I'll see you there about nine thirty?"

"Count on it, Katy. Thanks for ringing."

After hanging up, Lorne dropped another two pieces of bread in the toaster and reboiled the kettle. She tapped her foot impatiently for the next three minutes. Finally, she buttered the toast and poured the water onto the instant coffee and set off up the stairs.

Tony moaned as he propped himself up against the headboard. "How's your dad?"

Lorne kissed him lightly on the lips as she placed the tray in front of him. "He looks as bad as you. Crap, I wish I could stay at home today to look after you both, but I really need to give the girls my support. You understand, don't you?"

"Of course I do. I'll have this and move downstairs to the couch. That way I'll be near your father if he needs me."

Lorne stripped off and put her mucky clothes in the washing basket. "I could call next door to see if the neighbour would pop in periodically during the day."

"I'll be fine. Don't fret."

She knew he was ill because his gaze stayed focused on her face instead of roaming her naked body like it usually did. "It's all very well saying that, but we need to make sure your wound isn't infected. You might think you're suffering from what Dad has, but we also have to consider your wound, too. I'll call the doctor during the day, see if he can come out and see you both."

He tore at a piece of toast and chewed it for a second or two. "You worry too much."

She waggled her backside at him and ran into the bathroom. After showering, she dressed in her black skirt suit, the one she hadn't worn since leaving the force. It felt both strange and invigorating at the same time. To her, wearing a suit was a statement of power. She hoped she could recapture the way she felt as a policewoman today. It was important for her to show her strength of character to boost her client's morale. They would be frightened by the day's events. She prayed that the court case wouldn't last longer than a day or two. The longer it was drawn out, the more the girl's nerves would likely be torn to shreds.

"Did you hear me?" Tony's voice brought her out of her reverie.

"Sorry, hon. I was miles away." She stepped into her shoes and walked over to the bed.

"That much is evident. I said you look amazing. At least, you will once you comb and dry your hair."

"Damn. I knew I'd forget something. Oh, and thanks for the compliment." She tore off her jacket and blow-dried her hair. "How's that?"

"Much better. Now give me a kiss, then go knock 'em dead."

Lorne kissed his lips and stroked his damp hair back off his forehead. "I still feel bad about leaving you."

"Nonsense. Take the tray for me, would you?"

"Of course. Would you like me to help you down the stairs?"

Tony shook his head. "You go. I'll manage. What time will you be back tonight?"

"I suppose around six thirty to sevenish. Shall I pick up a take-away?"

"Might be an idea. Not sure your dad and I will be up to much. We could share one, maybe."

"Good idea. See you later."

Lorne left the bedroom and took his breakfast tray downstairs, then went to pick up her father's breakfast dish. He had half nibbled at his toast but had managed to eat all of his cereal. She told him that Tony was going to spend the day on the sofa, so he'd be close at hand.

Lorne quickly rinsed the breakfast things and left the house five minutes later.

She was halfway into London before she realized she hadn't drunk or eaten anything herself all morning. You'll have to wait till later, stomach.

Lorne's heart was racing as she approached the city. Thankfully, the traffic was much lighter than she'd anticipated, and she made it to the courthouse with five minutes to spare. She parked in the multi-storey car park a few streets away and trotted in her high heels to meet the others.

On the steps of the old courthouse, she found the three girls waiting for her. Lorne had telephoned Fiona a few days before and instructed her on what the girls should wear. Both Ami and Linda had chosen to wear black trouser suits, while Fiona wore a cherry-coloured tailored skirt suit that stopped just below the knee.

"Hi. How is everyone doing?" Lorne asked as she came to a stop beside Fiona.

"We've been better," Fiona replied her smile a little strained.

"We're on the final stretch. Stay strong and focused, and we'll make it over the finish line together." Lorne heard footsteps behind her and turned anxiously. She blew out a relieved breath when Katy joined them.

"Bloody hell, I thought I was going to be late," a breathless Katy said.

Lorne smiled and patted her on the arm. "I've only just arrived, myself. I'm so glad you could make it, Katy."

"You can thank Sean later. I put in extra hours last week, so I could have the day off today."

"We can't thank you enough for both being here. Without your support, we couldn't have made it this far," Linda said, her eyes a little misty. Both Ami and Fiona nodded their agreement.

"What happens now?" Fiona asked.

"Why don't we talk inside—"

A commotion behind them interrupted Lorne. She turned to see a jostling crowd approaching the courthouse. In the centre was the smug-looking Gibson. To his left were a tall grey-haired gentleman and an elegant, thin lady. To his right was his solicitor, his QC, dressed in all his finery and ready for action. Surrounding them were at least twenty to thirty journalists and photographers.

"Okay, let's get inside before this turns into a media circus." Lorne ushered the bewildered girls through the entrance and towards a row of seats at the end of the long panelled corridor with a high-vaulted ceiling. Terror emanated from Ami and Linda's eyes as their gaze darted between the entrance and Lorne.

"I know it's difficult, and I'd hate to be in your shoes, but please don't let him get to you. I know you well enough to know that your inner strength and courage will get you through this ordeal. Don't let the bastard intimidate you.

"This is what's going to happen: Gibson will go through to the courtroom and be placed in the dock. As witnesses, Ami and Linda, you will have to remain outside until you're called to give evidence. Fiona, you have the choice to either remain out here or sit in court and listen to the proceedings."

They all turned to see the group of journalists pile through the door before the court ushers pounced and shooed the press back outside onto the street.

Linda's hands clutched at Ami's, despite Lorne's warning to remain calm. It was to be expected given the circumstances, but as Lorne glanced over at Gibson, she saw laughter gathering momentum in his eyes as he watched them. You'll get yours, mister. You're so cock-sure of yourself, right now. Let's see what your reaction is going to be like once you're sitting in the dock.

Fiona leaned forward and whispered, "That can't be right, can it? Him being in the same area as us? The girls are going to start freaking out in a minute, and who could blame them? Can't you do something, Lorne?"

"It's just the way it is, Fiona. There's not a lot I—or anyone—can do. If Gibson were still in custody, he would have been taken up into court via the court cells. At the moment, he's deemed a free man; he has as much right to be in this area as we do. We'll just have to keep the girls distracted until the case starts."

Fiona nodded. "Easier said than done, I think. I'll do my best."

"We all will. Katy, are you going to stay out here with us or sit in court?"

Katy was staring at Gibson as she answered, "I think one of us should be in there. I'd like to see how the little shit reacts when the charges are read out."

"Agreed. I'll stay with the girls. We can have a chat over lunch." Lorne watched a timid brunette in her thirties walk through the entrance. The girl immediately changed direction and started to walk back out of the building when she laid eyes on Gibson. The middle-aged woman accompanying the girl slung a protective arm around her shoulder and guided the girl towards Lorne and the others. "I think she must be the other victim."

Katy acknowledged the woman with a brief wave. "Yep, that's her. Cally Little. I'll just go and have a quick word with her." She went over to Cally.

"Can't she come and join us?" Fiona asked, a sympathetic look on her face as she studied the girl's demeanour.

"Best not to. They don't advise witnesses sitting together during a trial. We'd only be giving the defence counsel ammunition. It's going to be tough enough for Ami and Linda in there, as it is. We don't want to jeopardise the case further by getting involved with the other witnesses."

"Gosh, I never thought of that. So you think Ami and Linda are going to suffer in there?" Fiona asked quietly so the other girls didn't hear.

"We all knew it wasn't going to be easy, Fiona, what with Ami living with you. Let's hope the jury doesn't think the girls' stories are made up. It's up to Ami and Linda to try and convince them that they're telling the truth."

Suddenly the large wooden doors to the courtroom were pushed open, and the usher called Gibson's name. The first thing Gibson did was glare in their direction. His eyes sought out Ami and Linda, and he gave them a cold hard stare before the elegant woman, presumably Gibson's mother, tugged at his arm and issued a few choice words.

The two girls, whose lives had been brutally affected by the callous man, each inhaled a harsh breath. Lorne turned to see them clinging to each other, their faces drained of all colour.

The pain and anxiety showing in their faces hurt Lorne. No matter what she said to try to comfort them, the girls were clearly terrified of Gibson and what they were about to encounter.

"Come on, you two. Don't let him get to you. I know it's difficult, but if you show him he has little effect on you, it'll unnerve him. My advice would be not to look in his direction when you step into the witness box. Katy will be in there to support you. Look at her, the jury, the prosecutor, or the defence solicitor. Do not look Gibson's way, agreed?"

Ami and Linda nodded their agreement as the usher of the court called Cally Little's name. The woman and her mother stood and walked towards the court. Cally hesitated for a moment before she pushed her shoulders back and marched into the courtroom. Her mother waited a few moments before she walked in after her.

"That's my cue to get in there, I think," Katy said. She brushed down her skirt and set off.

"See you at lunchtime," Lorne called out after her.

The morning dragged by. Lorne paced the flag-stoned corridor virtually the whole time as she waited for Cally to emerge from court. The three girls didn't utter a single word, each of them lost in her own terrified thoughts.

Finally, at twelve fifteen, the court doors were thrown open, and a small crowd of people surged out. As Katy marched towards them, Lorne noticed a tearful Cally come out of the court, her mum's arm wrapped tightly around her shoulders, comforting her. Well, that doesn't bode well.

"There's a café around the corner; let's grab some lunch," Lorne stated when Katy joined them.

Reluctantly the three girls followed Katy and Lorne out the entrance into the bustling street, where the press pounced on them. With the three girls between them, Katy and Lorne pushed through the predatory press pack.

"Come on, girls. Give us your side of what happened?" shouted one of the journalists.

"No comment. You know better than to ask such foolish questions," Lorne responded harshly. "Leave us alone, and go pester the defendant instead."

"Thought you had left the force, Simpkins. What brings you here?" asked a journalist Lorne knew well and disliked intensely.

"These ladies are friends of mine. Now, if you don't mind."

Recognising they weren't going to get any gossip out of the group, the crowd quickly dispersed.

Lorne pushed open the café door and let out a relieved sigh. From the girls' appearances, the press experience had shaken them up pretty badly.

She ordered bacon rolls and coffees for all five of them, then joined the others at the table. She tried her hardest to make small talk, but no one was really interested in engaging in futile conversation. Whilst eating her bacon roll, she asked Katy quietly, "How's it looking in there?"

Katy swallowed what she was chewing and frowned. "To be honest, it's not what I was expecting at all."

"Oh, in what way?" Lorne took another bite of her roll; she was hungrier than she thought, after missing her breakfast.

"Gibson's playing a crafty game."

Lorne quickly glanced over at the other girls to see if they'd heard. They hadn't. "What do you mean?"

"I reckon his solicitor has told him to try to gain the jury's sympathy. When Cally was giving her evidence, I would've expected him to look arrogant and to try to intimidate her in some way, but he didn't. To me, he looked the picture of innocence."

Lorne drew in a heavy breath. "Damn. All we can hope for is that his little plan backfires in some way. Is Cally returning to the stand after lunch?"

Katy took a sip of coffee. "I think so. The poor thing is finding it tough up there. His solicitor is tearing her statement to pieces."

"There was another witness to her attack though, wasn't there?"

"Yeah. I'm not sure if the guy is here or not. I haven't seen him." Katy wrinkled her nose.

"If he isn't called, that could seriously damage our case," Lorne said, worried.

CHAPTER SEVENTEEN

Court resumed promptly at two, and poor Cally Little was called to take the stand again. After half an hour, a distraught Cally came running out of the court, barged past a few people who were waiting by the entrance, and fled into the street.

Lorne glanced at the three girls, all of whom were sitting wide-eyed in fear. Before she had the chance to reassure them, the usher shouted Linda's name. Linda covered her mouth with a shaking hand.

Fiona grabbed it, and pulled Linda to her feet. "Don't crumble, sweetheart. This is your opportunity to get this man off the streets. Think of that, please."

"Listen to your sister, Linda. Think positively, tell the truth, and justice will prevail. Good luck. Fiona will be with you every step; Katy is inside too. Remember what I said: Don't look at him." Lorne pecked Linda on the cheek as the usher called her name for a second time.

If Lorne didn't know any better, she would have said that Linda was on the verge of passing out, all colour had drained from her face, there was a dazed look in her eyes, and her legs seemed to be unsteady. Serious doubts were beginning to gather momentum in Lorne's mind about if either Linda or Ami would be able to go through with the torment of court, after all.

Fiona escorted Linda to the courtroom entrance and stood back for a count of three before she followed her in.

Lorne was dying to be inside the court, but she had to remain with Ami, who was shaking from head to toe, looking like the fight was evaporating with every breath she took and that she was capable of taking flight at any second. They sat side by side on the uncomfortable wooden bench, Lorne protectively clutching Ami's hand in her lap. She could feel the girl trembling, and her palm became sweatier by the minute.

About an hour later, Lorne could feel her phone vibrating in her jacket pocket. She removed it from her pocket and was surprised to see her home number being displayed. "Excuse me a minute."

She stood up and walked halfway up the hallway before answering, "Tony? Is that you?"

"Sorry, babe. I was just wondering how things are going?"

"It's okay. I'm outside the court with Ami. Linda's on the stand now. It's hard to tell how it's going in there, although Katy is suspicious of the way Gibson is behaving."

Tony snorted. "That figures. His QC would've told him to be on his best behaviour to try to gain the jury's sympathy. How are the girls holding up?"

"So-so. The other witness left the court about an hour ago in a terrible state. The girls were unnerved by Cally's reaction—Cally's the other witness. How are you feeling, sweetie?"

"A bit better. Tell the girls to stay strong. Oh, by the way, you had a visitor this morning."

"Sounds ominous. Was it someone wanting to rehome one of the dogs?"

"Kind of. A woman in her late forties—early fifties, maybe. She said she met you a few years back, helped you crack a serial killer case or something."

Lorne thought it over for the briefest of moments before the woman's picture filled her mind. "Oh, you mean Carol Lang, the psychic."

"That's the one. Seemed a little weird to me."

"Did she say what she wanted?" Lorne asked, turning to check how Ami was doing.

"Apparently her dog died last month. She saw the ad in the local at the weekend and recognised your name. I told her you'd be out all day, and she went all weird on me."

"Really? In what way?" The one and only time Lorne had met Ms Lang had been when Pete, her old work partner, had been alive. He had been a cynic and doubted Ms Lang's skills, which in the end had indeed helped solve the case in which Lorne was abducted by a serial killer. During one of her insightful visions, Carol Lang had passed out in Lorne's office. Now, that was weird.

"Well, after she told me off for not being tucked up in bed, she sort of went off on a tangent. Started omming, if you like. When I said you'd be back later this evening, she knew instantly where you were."

"Really? She knew I was in court, you mean?"

"Yep. Anyway, she wants to see you in person. She's going to call you this evening."

"Sounds mysterious, as usual. We'll find out what's up later, then. Go get some rest, love. Have you and Dad eaten lunch?"

"I heated up the soup you left in the pot. Your dad didn't eat much. I think we should call the doc out tomorrow if he's no better this evening. I'll let you go. Love you."

"Love you too, Tony. Get some rest." She blew her husband a kiss and hung up, then strolled casually back to Ami, who jumped when she sat down beside her.

"It's all right; it's only me. Sorry about that; Hubby was checking up on me." Lorne laughed, but Ami's face didn't even crack into a smile.

Ami's gaze returned to staring at the panelled wall opposite, and she looked lost in thought. Lorne struggled to gain her attention.

The rest of the afternoon dragged by. Finally, at four forty-five, the doors to the court opened, Linda and Fiona came marching up the hallway towards them. At first glance, Linda appeared fine; she didn't seem as though she'd been through any kind of ordeal in the past few hours. Fiona gave a half-smile, letting Lorne know that things had gone as well as expected.

Katy emerged with the rest of the crowd several minutes later.

Lorne rushed to meet her. "How did it go, Katy?"

"The defence counsel was far easier on Linda than I had anticipated. It's hard to tell what the hell they're playing at. Maybe they didn't see Linda as the easier target and they're saving all the shit for when Ami gets up there."

"Christ, I hope not. Linda is the stronger of the two. I'm not sure Ami is up for this, full stop. If I hadn't been with her this afternoon, I get the impression she would've bolted." Lorne motioned with her head for Katy to turn round.

Gibson and his QC had joined his parents at the other end of the hallway. Their demeanour—for all of them—was jovial.

As if he sensed Lorne was looking at him, Gibson turned in her direction, flashed his brilliant white teeth, and raised a confident eyebrow. The smarmy bag of shit. Lorne didn't often get bad vibes about a case. She was always one to think positive till the end, but something niggled in the pit of her stomach.

They waited for the gloating group to leave the courtroom before they attempted to go back to their cars. Again, they watched from the stone steps outside as the bustling press pack jostled Gibson's group.

Lorne urged the girls to hurry while the press were distracted. Lorne and Katy saw the girls back to their vehicle and waved them off.

"I'm afraid I won't be able to make it tomorrow, Lorne," Katy said as they went up a level in the car park to where both their cars were parked.

"I understand, Katy. I appreciate you coming here today. The girls did, too. Let's hope Ami has the courage to turn up tomorrow; I have my doubts."

Katy searched in her bag for her keys and unlocked her car. "She does look extremely fragile. Good luck with helping her keep it all together. I'll give you a ring tomorrow evening, about seven?"

"Thanks, Katy. Speak soon." Lorne watched Katy drive away before she sought out her own car, deep in thought.

Something pointed that felt like a gun was placed at the base of her spine. "Turn round, and you're dead, lady."

Lorne swallowed hard. Crap, you let your guard down. The gunman jabbed her, forcing her to move forward. Before long, they had reached the edge of the car park and the three-foot high wall. Her heart pounded as the voice told her to get up on the wall. She tried to turn, but the gun jabbed her hard in the spine. She cried out in pain.

"I said, get up on the wall," the man repeated angrily.

Lorne dropped her handbag on the floor beside her and attempted to climb the wall. She huffed and puffed, making out that she was struggling to reach it.

"Stop playing with me, Simpkins. Put some effort in, or I'll shoot you on the spot."

Think, girl. Think. She attempted a second time and tumbled back, wincing as the gun caught her in the kidney. "I can't do it."

She heard the gunman release a frustrated breath. "Hitch your fucking skirt up around your arse if you have to. Lost the ability to think properly since you left the Met, have you?"

Lorne knew she wouldn't be able to stall for time much longer. She hitched up her skirt and attempted to clamber on to the wall. She glanced over the edge and almost lost her stomach; a fifty-foot drop had the ability to affect a person like that.

With the gun no longer pressed in her back, her brain started to function better. She groaned with exertion as she pulled herself onto the wall. The man laughed behind her.

She took the opportunity to fall back against him. The gun clattered to the ground.

"What the fuck—"

Lorne kicked the gun under a nearby car, out of his reach, and flew at the masked man, her arms flailing in all directions.

He was slow to react, obviously lost without his gun to hide behind. A few karate chops landed on either side of his head. He cried out in pain and ran off.

"Come back here, you cowardly piece of shit," she screamed at his retreating back as he ran through the door that led to the stairwell. Getting down on all fours, she took a handkerchief from her bag and reached under the car to retrieve the gun.

She rang Katy. "Katy, it's me. Can you come back to the car park? Someone just tried to kill me," she said breathlessly from her exertions.

"What? I'm on my way."

CHAPTER EIGHTEEN

Lorne flinched when Katy's car screeched to a halt beside her. She raised her hand. "Calm down. I'm fine, honestly. I managed to disarm him. He ran off. No point chasing him; he'll be long gone by now."

"Jesus! Did you get a good look at him, Lorne?"

"Nope. He had a balaclava on. I have my suspicions, though." Lorne handed the wrapped gun to Katy.

Katy pulled back the handkerchief and had a peek at it. Shaking her head, she said, "Someone meant business. Who do you think it was?"

"Are you kidding me? Gibson, of course. It has to be."

Katy's face was full of uncertainty. "You think? The last we saw of him, he was walking away with his parents."

Lorne felt like pummelling the side of Katy's head. "Think about it, Katy—the threatening email and phone call. All right, I get your point, but it needn't have necessarily been him. He could've paid someone to attack me."

"I'm not so sure. Did the attacker say anything to make you think that? It might have just been an attempted mugging."

Lorne bit the inside of her cheek, trying to suppress her anger. "He used my name. He knew I used to work with the Met. I was definitely his intended target."

Katy gave an embarrassed shrug. "Oh! Will you be okay to get home? I better get this off to the lab to see if we can get any prints from it."

"I'll be fine. Any chance you can rush things through? We need to get this idiot locked up ASAP."

Katy opened her passenger door and deposited the gun on the seat. "I'll see what I can do. I can't make any promises, though. Be in touch soon," she added as she jumped in the driver's side. She waited until Lorne was settled in her own car before she drove off.

Lorne made the journey home on autopilot while her mind raced about what Gibson had done, if indeed the attacker had been him.

Lorne entered the lounge, gave Tony a quick kiss on the forehead, and collapsed on the sofa next to him.

"What's wrong?"

Lorne debated long and hard whether she should tell him about the incident in the car park or not before she answered. "Long day, that's all."

"I know when you're lying, hon. I may be under the weather, but my stupidity level hasn't risen. Besides, you promised to bring in a take-away, and I can't smell any food."

Lorne leapt out of the chair. "Damn! I knew I'd forgotten something."

Tony reached up and grabbed her hand. "Lorne, you're worrying me. I don't care about dinner. What's wrong?"

She knew it would be pointless keeping the truth from him. Because of his training, her husband was the type who resembled a dog digging for a damn bone if they didn't get the answer they were looking for. "After we came out of court, I said goodbye to the others, and..."

He tugged her back down next to him. "And?"

"I let my guard down, and someone attacked me from behind."

"What? Who?"

"Don't go getting worked up, Tony. I don't know who. He had a gun and tried to force me up on to the wall of the car park. I think his intention was to make me jump."

"Shit!" He threw the quilt back and staggered to his feet.

"What are you doing?" Lorne asked.

"I'm getting dressed. Then I'm going to drive over to that coward Gibson's house and see what he has to say for himself."

Lorne wasn't surprised that Tony had come to the same conclusion as she had. She stood up and gripped the top of his arms. "And what good will that do? I have no proof it was him. The attacker wore a balaclava, Tony. Katy's taken the gun back to dust for prints. Let's see what the results are first, huh?"

She touched the side of his face; his skin still felt clammy. "My hero. Always keen to jump to my defence, even if you're at death's door."

He leaned forward, and they shared a lingering kiss before he came up gasping for breath. "You know I'd never let anyone hurt you, love."

"I know that, sweetie. I'll just go see how Dad is, and then I'll nip out again for the fish and chips." She turned to walk out the door.

"If anything happened to you... I'd be finished."

She stopped and smiled reassuringly. "I doubt that. Besides, nothing is going to happen to me, so stop fretting."

"Forget the take-away, too. An omelette will suffice for me."

"I'll see how Dad is and then decide."

She went down the hallway to her father's room. His eyes were firmly closed, and his bare arms were outside the quilt, resting on the bed beside him. His pyjama jacket had been taken off and was lying on the floor next to the bed.

She didn't like the look of him. Perspiration dotted his forehead, and his skin was ashen. "Dad?" She approached the bed.

When her father didn't respond, she shook him gently. He groaned, but his eyes didn't open.

"Dad," she repeated, more loudly. He didn't respond.

She went to the hallway and called the doctor on her mobile. "Please hurry, Doctor. I'm deeply concerned about him."

"Settle down, Lorne. I'm sure it's nothing, Sam's heart is strong. I'll be there in ten minutes."

Tony came out of the lounge. "Shit! He was fine about half an hour ago, Lorne."

"I'm not blaming you, Tony. He looks really rough. The doc's on his way. I want him to take a look at you while he's here too; no arguments. We don't know what we're dealing with here."

"I can see where you're coming from. Maybe we should have had some kind of shots before we started up this place."

"You think he—you've both—picked up a disease from the dogs?" Lorne asked devastated. If that was the case she'd put her whole family at an unnecessary risk.

"Who knows? We take in strays; half the time we don't know what they've been exposed to."

Lorne shook her head. "I don't think so, Tony. The vet always gives them a clean bill of health, remember? No, I'm sure the dogs aren't connected with this. Before we jump to conclusions, let's see what the doc has to say, eh?" She went through to the kitchen to make a coffee while they waited for the doctor to arrive.

His ten minutes turned out to be almost twenty. Lorne paced the kitchen floor, running a frantic hand through her hair.

She heard the doctor's car crunch its way up the gravel driveway and yanked the kitchen door open. "Oh, thank heavens."

"Sorry, there was an accident up the road. A lorry had spilt its load, and I had to take a detour," Doctor Darwin apologised, rushing into the house with his medical bag in his right hand. The doctor followed Lorne through to her father's room.

"Both Tony and Dad have been bad the last few days. I've been in court all day. I had every intention of ringing you, but something came up, and it completely went out of my mind. When I got home, I checked on Dad, and he seemed a lot worse," she explained, watching as the doctor checked her father's blood pressure and pulse.

"Sam. Can you hear me?" the doctor asked as he placed a hand on her father's forehead. Her father let out a moan.

With his examination over, the doctor motioned for Lorne to join him out in the hallway. Tony who had been lingering by the door backed up a little to give them room.

"What is it?" Lorne asked anxiously.

"I don't want to worry you, but your father has a rash. I hope I'm wrong, but I think we could be looking at a case of meningitis, Lorne."

"Oh my God." All her strength seemed to have been sapped out of her, and she collapsed against the wall.

Tony rushed to her side. "What does that mean exactly, Doc?"

"There are several different types of meningitis. Let's get him to hospital and see which type we're dealing with. I'll ring for an ambulance. Can you gather a few things for him? You know, the usual for a few days' stay." The doctor turned, and with his mobile attached to his ear, he walked through the kitchen and out to his car to finish the call.

"Lorne, now don't start panicking. Sam's in safe hands."

"Easier said than done. I should've thought about calling the doc earlier. I've been so distracted lately." She smashed her clenched fists against her thighs.

Tony held out his arms, and she walked into them. He smoothed a hand down her hair and kissed her forehead with gentle kisses. How had she ever managed without him?

The doctor reappeared and walked past them to check on her father. "The ambulance is on its way. Can you tell me what Sam's symptoms have been over the past few days?"

"He's been a bit sniffly, off his food, complaining of a headache. I just thought it was a slight cold or some bug he'd caught. We even thought of the possibility that he'd picked up something from the dogs."

The doctor shook his head briskly. "Highly unlikely that would be the case. Treated with caution, meningitis isn't contagious, but close contact should be avoided at all times. It's doubtful either of you will catch it. That's why we need to get him into hospital."

She looked over her shoulder, at Tony resting against the doorframe. "That's reassuring, because Tony has been feeling a bit rough for a day or two also."

"I think I'll check you out all the same, Tony. Any problems with the leg? An infection, maybe?" The doctor motioned for Tony to sit in her father's easy chair next to the bed.

He took Tony's blood pressure and checked his pulse, and he didn't look particularly disturbed by his findings. Then he knelt on the floor and rolled up Tony's pyjama trousers and studied his injured leg. Tony winced when the doctor felt his stump.

"Yep, I think it's a little infected. I'll give you a course of antibiotics; that should clear it up in no time at all."

"Well, that's a relief." Lorne ruffled Tony's hair. "Sorry, I mean it's bad enough, but at least it's not something more serious." Her gaze drifted over to her father, and she blinked away the mistiness that briefly clouded her vision.

She heard a siren in the distance and sprinted around the room, gathering her father's essentials together. She searched the bottom of his wardrobe, pulled out his overnight bag, and shoved everything in it.

Soon her unconscious father was placed in a wheelchair and wheeled out to the ambulance. "I'll give you a call from the hospital," she called back to Tony as she clambered in the back and sat in the chair nearest to her father's head. "Damn, will you ring Jade for me?"

* * *

After several hours of tests, the conclusion was that her father did indeed have viral meningitis. There was little the hospital could do for him as far as medication was concerned, for antibiotics wouldn't help fight the disease. Her father would need to stay in hospital for a few days of bed rest where his progress would be monitored. That was a relief to Lorne, once she realised her workload had just multiplied, what with having two invalids on her hands.

Her distraught sister had arrived and was sitting by their father's bed, holding his hand.

She left Jade and went to the entrance of the hospital to get some fresh air and make some calls on her mobile. "Tony. Just a quick one. Dad's going to be okay. It is what the doc thought."

"Shit! But he's going to get through it, right?"

"It needs to run its course. He's going to stay in hospital for a few days. Look, I'll stay here for a few hours with Jade, in case he wakes up and wonders where he is."

"No problem. Give Jade a hug for me. Try to grab something to eat from the machine or the canteen. You'll need to keep your strength up. Love you."

"I'll get us both a sandwich, if I get the chance. See you later. Love you, too."

The second call, she dreaded making. "Fiona? It's Lorne. Did you get home all right?"

"Hi, Lorne. Yeah, we did, thanks. You?" Fiona sounded distracted, and pans rattled in the background, as if Lorne had disturbed their dinner preparations.

"Ah, that's why I'm ringing. I'm at the hospital—"

"What? Why? What's happened?" The background noise instantly stopped, and Fiona gave her full attention.

"When I got home, my dad was really ill. The doctor called the ambulance, and he was admitted to hospital, straight away."

"Oh, no. Sorry to hear that. Nothing too serious, I hope?"

While she was talking Lorne glanced around the car park. One car in particular caught her eye—a black Range Rover. The tinted windows obscured her view of the driver. The car was inching back and forwards, as if to tease her. Lorne started to approach it, but it sped off when she was within two feet of the back door. "Damn," she said under her breath before she replied to Fiona's question. "Serious enough. Viral meningitis. Not sure how to say this, but I'm not going to be able to be in court tomorrow with you guys."

She heard Fiona suck in a breath. "Hey, that's completely understandable. Family comes first, Lorne. I'll tell the other girls. We'll be there to support Ami, anyway. Thanks for letting me know. Hope your dad gets better soon."

"Thanks. I'll try to ring tomorrow, either during the day or in the evening, to see how things went." She looked over at the entrance and saw the same car going backwards and forwards a few times. She pressed the end call button on her phone, then placed yet another call. "Katy, it's me."

"Christ, what's wrong now? Hang on; let me get my shoes on while we talk."

"Don't bother. I'm at the hospital." She quickly added, "I'm all right. Dad's ill, though. Look, that's not why I'm ringing. I'm in the car park at the hospital, and I keep seeing this strange car. If I didn't know any better, I'd say the driver was keeping an eye on me. Of course, after what happened earlier, there's a possibility I'm being more than a little bit paranoid."

"Crap! Did you manage to take note of the plate number?"

"Yep." She gave Katy the number and watched the car come to a standstill outside the hospital gates again. "The bastard drove off when I walked up to the car, but he's sitting at the gates now, taunting me."

"I'll ring the station get them to check who it belongs to. I'll also see if I can get a patrol car over there to scare him off. Ring back in five minutes or so."

"I'll be waiting," Lorne said, focusing on the car once more.

A few minutes later, her phone jangled the CSI theme tune. She answered it. "Hi. What did you find out?"

"You won't be surprised when you hear who the vehicle is registered to. You know what? I've had it with Gibson. I'm going to ring the prosecutor and see what he makes of this harassment."

"Thanks, Katy. You're a treasure. The girls are going it alone tomorrow; I hope they'll be okay."

"Okay, I get the message. I'll have a word with Roberts in the morning, see if I can grab an hour or so off."

"Katy, have I told you lately how wonderful you are?"

"Hmm... Let's see how things work out before you start heaping praise on me. Take care. Give your father a kiss from me."

They both hung up. Lorne glanced over at the gates to see the Range Rover drive off. A second or two later, a police car drove by, going in the same direction.

Nice to see my contacts are still capable of making a difference.

Lorne and Jade stayed with their unconscious father for another two hours before the nurse ordered them to go home. "We'll call you if your father wakes up. Go home and get some rest, yourselves. You both look done in."

Lorne smiled and nodded at the pretty brunette nurse who had been put in charge of her dad. "I feel it. Not sure about Jade. You'll ring us as soon as he wakes up?"

"Of course. Don't worry; he's in good hands. Leave your number at reception on your way out, if you would."

After leaving her number, Lorne stepped out into the chilly night air and walked Jade to her car. Her sister had barely said two words to her since arriving at the hospital, and she couldn't help wondering if Jade wasn't blaming her for her father's illness.

Lorne decided it wasn't the time to have it out with her. She waved her sister off and sought out her own vehicle, scanning all around her, alert and ready for a possible attack.

On the drive home, her stomach groaned, crying out for the meal she had missed. She stopped at the local chip shop and then rushed home to share the fish supper with Tony. Neither of them had much of an appetite, and they both picked at the meal.

Halfway through their dinner, the house phone rang. Lorne answered it. "Hello?" she asked anxiously, expecting the call to be from the hospital.

"Lorne, how lovely to hear your voice."

She wracked her brain, trying to figure out where she had heard the familiar voice before. Then she remembered what Tony had said earlier in the day, and it dawned on her who the mystery caller had to be. "Carol. How have you been? Long time, no hear."

"Ah, you remembered. I'm as well as can be expected, I suppose. I dropped by earlier and chatted with your husband. Nice man—so much better than your last one. Not that I met him, of course. But I can tell you two are much better suited."

Lorne chuckled, and Tony frowned at her. She mouthed at him, "I'll tell you later."

She turned her attention back to Carol, "Tony said you were after another dog. It's so sad when we lose a beloved pet."

"Yes, my Totty was the love of my life. I thought this time I would give a homeless dog a new home rather than buy a pedigree. Imagine my surprise when I saw your name on the advert in the local paper. Umm... I was sorry to read about your partner a few years back, Lorne. I know he and I never saw eye to eye, but I could tell his heart was in the right place. I read his aura, you know. It was ninety percent good. He idolised you. I think that's why he acted the way he did towards me—he was trying to protect you."

Unexpected tears threatened to spill, and Lorne coughed to clear the lump that had formed in her throat. "I still miss him today, Carol."

"There's no need, dear. He's watching over you every hour of the day."

"That's good to know. Listen, I've had a hectic day. Why don't you call by and see me tomorrow? I'll be here all day."

"That'd be lovely. I'll pick up a couple of sumptuous cakes from the baker's up the road and be there about eleven. I didn't think you'd be able to go to court, with your father so ill. He'll be all right, dear. It's God's way of telling him to slow down. I need to have a chat with you about the case you're working on, anyway."

Lorne sat up, intrigued. "That's reassuring about Dad, thanks, Carol. Umm… What can you tell me about the case?"

"All will be revealed tomorrow, dear, over a nice pot of tea and a cream cake. Cheerio for now."

Lorne hung up and stared at the phone for a long moment before she put it back down on the table beside the sofa. "Well, that was weird."

"I told you she went weird earlier. What did she say?"

She shrugged. "Not a lot. She said all will be revealed tomorrow."

CHAPTER NINETEEN

The following morning, Lorne greeted Carol Lang with a hug. The woman hadn't changed a bit, apart from the few stray grey hairs streaking through her long black hair. She still wore the long flowing black witchlike outfit she'd worn the first day Lorne had met her in her office at the station.

She showed the woman into the kitchen. Carol placed a cake box on the kitchen table and studied her intently. "You look happier, my dear. I mean, despite all your problems at the moment—which will all blow over, soon enough."

"Thanks, Carol. I am." Lorne glanced up at Tony, who was standing in the doorway. "I can thank my husband for that."

"Indeed. He's a good man in spite of his questionable past," Carol said, shaking her head and crinkling her eyes as unwanted images seemed to be running through her mind.

Tony gave Lorne an amused smile and raised an eyebrow as if to say, 'What have I been telling you all these months?'

"All right, Carol. Don't beef his part up. His head won't be able to fit through the door soon."

They all laughed, but then Carol suddenly stopped. "How are the girls holding up, Lorne?"

"By girls, are you talking about the girls concerned with the case we are working on?" The serious expression on the psychic's face caused Lorne's heart rate to increase.

"Yes. I'm worried for them. They have gentle, almost angelic souls, but this man has destroyed them in immeasurable ways." Carol sat down in one of the chairs at the kitchen table.

"To be honest, I'm worried about them. The guy involved is a nasty piece of work. I'm so concerned for their well-being that I've actually given one of our dogs to the girls to help protect them," Lorne admitted.

"Blackie is a sweetheart, and he is caring for them well. But it's not enough. I think you need to keep a close eye on them—a very close eye, just to be on the safe side."

Lorne and Tony both pulled out a chair and sat on either side of Carol. Lorne asked, "What have you seen, Carol?"

"It's been a little fuzzy up till now, dear. But I've seen enough to know that the girls' problems aren't finished. This man needs watching. He's hatching a plan to get even with the girls." Carol placed the fingertips of both her hands on her forehead above each eye and fell silent for a nanosecond. "I must tell you, you wouldn't think to look at him, but he's an extremely dangerous man. Of course you're aware of that already, after today's events. The problem is he has influential people in high places, people who will do everything in their power to get him out of a hole. He's found himself in countless holes over the years." She shook her head in disgust.

"I'll tell the girls to be extra vigilant, then. Crumbs, how do I tell them that without scaring them?"

"Blackie's presence will help to reassure the girls, but..." Carol drifted off, closed her eyes and started rocking in her chair. "I don't like the look of this. Ring the girls, Lorne, immediately."

Lorne looked up at the kitchen clock it was just before eleven. "I can't. They'll be in court. Ami is due to give evidence today against Gibson. What is it, Carol?"

"You know I haven't let you down in the past, Lorne. Trust me when I say that Gibson will get off and he'll be hell bent on exacting his revenge on the girls for dragging his name through the mud."

"My God, what will he do? Shit, what can we do to help the girls?"

Carol let out a long shuddering breath. "You've done all you can to protect them." She paused, reached across the table, and clutched Lorne's hand in her own clammy hand. "I'm sorry, but Blackie is no longer with us."

Lorne snatched her hand back. "What? What do you mean—that he's dead, Carol?"

The woman nodded, and tears welled up in her black kohl–rimmed eyes. "The girls have no idea. They'll go home this evening to find him dead. I'm so sorry."

Lorne looked over at Tony, who was shaking his head and eyeing Carol sceptically. "Can we get this vision verified first, before we start worrying the girls?" Tony asked.

"It's true, I tell you; but if you doubt my abilities, by all means, check it out. Can you go to the girls' flat? While they're in court, I mean."

She'd have to live for years with the guilt of placing Blackie in danger. That poor defenceless dog. How anyone could possibly kill a dog sickened and angered Lorne. "I'll drive over there." She rose from the table, frantic, and her legs almost gave way beneath her.

Tony stood up and caught her in his arms. "I'm not letting you go anywhere in that state, love." Turning to Carol, he asked, "Are you positive about this?"

Carol nodded and stood up, too. "As sure as day follows night in the circle of life. If you want to go over there, Lorne, we can go together. I'll drive you."

"I have to go, Tony. To see for myself. Would you, Carol? That'd be so kind of you. I'll need to ring the hospital first to see how Dad is."

Tony bent to kiss her on the cheek. "Leave the hospital to me. I'll ring while you get yourself ready."

"Thanks, hon. Carol, I'll be ready in five minutes." With regained strength, Lorne ran out of the room. Upstairs in the bedroom, she changed her clothes for the third time that morning. She put on another set of clean working clothes, thinking that she wouldn't want to ruin her best jeans if she had cause to climb the fence at the girls' flat.

* * *

Approximately five minutes later, Lorne and Carol set off.

The midday autumn sun filled the car with warmth. Despite that, Lorne couldn't prevent the shudders from making her twitch.

"I'm sorry, Lorne," Carol said quietly.

"I feel so guilty now, for placing Blackie there. All he ever wanted was a home, a decent home he could feel settled in. Now this. I'm not disbelieving you, Carol, but just this once, I hope your vision proves to be wrong."

Carol let out a long breath. "So do I. Hey, we need to have a chat later about me adopting one of your strays. That was the real reason behind my visit today. I had no idea this was in the cards."

"Of course. I'm sorry. I'd love you to have one of the dogs. I know it will be well cared for. Actually, I think I have just the dog for you: a Yorkie whose owner had to go in a nursing home. Nelly came in last week. I'll introduce you when we get back if you like?"

"Another small dog sounds ideal. I wasn't really after a large dog." Carol fed the steering wheel through her hands to manoeuvre around the upcoming roundabout.

"One thing is puzzling me, Carol. When you rang last night, you hinted that you wanted to chat about the case. Did you see Blackie's demise then?"

"Goodness, no! I would've told you something like that instantly. No, I mainly wanted to warn you that the girls need to be aware of this man. A word of caution: I'm not sure you should discuss with them what I told you about him being found not guilty. You never know how people will react to news they don't want to hear."

"I understand. We'll keep it between us for now."

"You know if I can be of any help in the future with any cases, you only have to shout." Carol glanced sideways at Lorne and smiled the briefest of smiles.

Wow! What an outfit we would be—an ex-DI, an invalid former MI6 agent, a retired ex-DCI, my teenage daughter, and a psychic.

"I'll bear it in mind. Thanks, Carol." Lorne pointed ahead of her. "The road we want is the next turning on your left."

Carol turned into the road and awaited further instructions.

"This is the house." Before Carol could apply the handbrake, Lorne had leapt out of the car and was bolting down the alley that ran alongside the side of the flat. She searched the fence for a possible weak panel to gain access to the garden. There wasn't one; all she found was a hole approximately five inches round, too small for anyone to fit through. There was no other option left open to her than to climb the fence.

She moved over to where two of the panels met and joined to a post and pulled herself up on to the top of the fence, where she balanced precariously for a second or two before she dropped down onto the grass on the other side. She ran over to the patio doors.

Peering through the window, she spotted Blackie lying prostrate on the living room floor. His eyes were wide open. There was blood and foamy saliva around his mouth and on the floor close to his head.

Lorne followed her first instinct to knock on the window to see if there was any reaction from the dog. Nothing.

Suspecting he'd been poisoned, Lorne retraced her steps and searched the garden for any incriminating evidence. Finally, by the gap in the fence she'd discovered earlier, she found a few scraps of beef.

"Lorne. Are you there?" Carol called from the other side of the fence.

"Do you have a plastic bag on you, Carol? A carrier bag, anything like that?"

"Yes, I have one in the car. I'll be right back." Lorne heard Carol's footsteps quicken and fade on the concrete path; moments later, she heard them increase again with the woman's return. Lorne put her hand through the gap and wiggled it. "Here, Carol."

The bag rustled as Lorne picked up the remnants of what she perceived to have been Blackie's final meal. Then she scrambled back over the fence, landing safely back on the other side. Holding up the bag, she said, "I think he was poisoned. Any chance you can give me a lift to the station?"

"Sure thing. Jump in. That poor creature; he suffered terribly. I wouldn't share that with the girls if I were you. They'll feel as guilty as you do."

"I can't help it. He was such a sweetheart. Can you remember the way?"

"I know he was. I think I can remember the way."

They arrived at the station about half an hour later. Carol remained in the car while Lorne ran inside.

The officer on the front desk greeted her like an old friend. "Ms Simpkins. How nice to see you again."

"Hello, John. I'm in kind of a hurry. Is DS Katy Foster around?"

He grimaced. "She left about five minutes ago. Can I help at all?"

"What about DCI Roberts—is he here?"

"Just a sec." He picked up the phone and dialled. "I've got DI Simpkins here, sir. She'd like a word with you, if it's convenient." He paused, then said, "Righto, sir. I'll tell her."

Lorne looked at the desk sergeant hopefully.

He nodded. "He'll be right down, ma'am… I mean, Lorne."

"Fantastic." She paced the area until Sean Roberts entered the room.

Everything appeared to stop for a minute or two as they stared at each other as she still felt guilty about walking away from his team.

"Lorne, you're looking good, girl." Sarcasm coloured his voice, and his gaze roamed over her unfashionable work clothes.

She held her arms out to the side and shrugged. "I guess you would call this my new uniform."

Roberts smiled. "What can I do for you?"

Lorne held up the carrier bag.

"I hope that's not what I think it is." He sniffed the air.

She lifted her gaze to the ceiling in mock annoyance, and he laughed.

"No. It isn't. Seriously, chief."

He raised an eyebrow, prompting her to correct herself.

"Sorry, Sean. Any chance you can get this analysed for me? The case I'm working on—the rape case—I just found my clients' dog dead. I found this at the scene, suspected poisoning."

"Bloody hell. I'll get on it straight away and ask them to get the results back ASAP. I'll ring you later." Roberts said to Lorne's back, as she was already halfway out the door.

"Thanks, Sean. You're my saviour. Gotta fly. Dad's in hospital," Lorne called back, using her father's illness as a means of a quick getaway.

"Wait. Why?" he shouted after her.

"I'll tell you later." Lorne jumped back in Carol's car, and they headed home. They were both silent for a while until Carol jolted her out of her contemplation.

"The girls will still need protection once he gets off the charges, Lorne."

"In the next few days, we should know what will happen. I'll have a word with my contact in the force to see if she can organise a patrol car to cruise the area as a deterrent."

"Mark my words: He's going to get off, either today or tomorrow. He won't be foolish enough to go back to their home again after what happened to Blackie. He'll try to set a trap for one of them."

"Damn, I better ring Fiona when we get back to pre-warn her about Blackie. The girls are going to be shit scared after this."

"How can we tell them to be careful without them worrying?" Carol asked, glancing sideways at Lorne.

"I don't see how we can. Oh, God, what a bloody mess."

CHAPTER TWENTY

Tony was incensed when Lorne told him how Blackie had died. He kicked the chair in the kitchen with his good leg and swore. "Fucking hell! If I get my hands on that bastard..."

Lorne ran a hand down his arm. "I'm gutted, too. I know this sounds harsh, but at the moment we have to brush Blackie's death to one side and focus on helping—or should I say protecting—the girls."

"Sorry. You're right. What about having a word with Katy or Roberts to get them police protection?" He retrieved the chair he'd just kicked and threw himself into it.

Lorne shook her head dejectedly. "They won't be eligible for that."

"Do you think he did it personally? Or do you think he paid someone else to do it?" Tony asked, looking from Lorne to Carol.

Lorne shrugged, but Carol nodded. "He did it, most definitely. Heartless through and through, that one. Extremely dangerous, too. I know I keep saying that, but it's the truth."

Lorne slumped into a kitchen chair, put her elbows on the, table and rested her head on her clenched fists. "I just don't know where we go from here," she said in a defeated tone.

"You can pack that in," Tony retorted. "I've never known you to give up on something, Lorne. We'll think of something. All's not lost. The jury might still find him guilty." He glanced at Carol, who was vehemently shaking her head. "Let's wait and see. You need to ring the girls immediately. I wonder if Fiona will give us a key. We could get Blackie out of there before the other girls see him."

Lorne smiled at her husband and felt blessed to have him around to guide her in her newfound uncertain world. "Let me ring her and see." She left the room and rang Fiona from the lounge. The young woman's mobile rang and rang before it finally went into voicemail. She left a message. "Fiona, it's Lorne. Please ring as soon as you get this message. It's very important."

Tony looked up expectantly when she walked back heavy footed into the kitchen. "Voicemail. Next idea?"

"Let's check on how your father is. Then we'll go over to the courthouse and get hold of Fiona that way," Tony said, seemingly pleased as his rusty brain notched up a gear.

"Sounds like a plan, but you're forgetting one thing."

Tony raised a questioning eyebrow.

Lorne swept her arm open. "This place. After what happened with Blackie, I'm not keen on leaving the kennels unattended. I know Gibson's in court at the moment, but you never know if he has an accomplice helping him do his dirty work."

"He hasn't, but I'll stay here," Carol offered with a smile. "It'll be my pleasure, Lorne."

"We couldn't impose on you like that."

"Nonsense. I have a free day today. Be off with you." Carol shooed the pair of them out the back door.

Lorne fired off instructions over her shoulder. "Just make sure the dogs have enough water. No need to let them out; I'll exercise them when we get back. Thanks, Carol."

Once in the car and with Tony driving, she rang the hospital. The ward sister reassured her that her father had slept well during the night and that his vital signs had showed a vast improvement. But they still wanted to keep him in for observation, for a day or two, at least.

* * *

Lorne ran up the steps to the courtroom faster than Sylvester Stallone in the Rocky film. Inside, she glanced down the corridor to where she had sat the day before with the girls and saw Linda sitting there with a girl she didn't know. Out of breath, Lorne asked, "Hi, Linda. Is Fiona around?"

"Lorne, what on earth are you doing here?"

"It's a long story. Is Fiona here?" Lorne repeated. She smiled and tried to keep her voice calm, not wishing to cause Linda any unnecessary alarm.

Linda motioned with her head towards the door to the court. "Ami's on the stand; Fiona is in there, giving her moral support."

"Thanks, I'll try to grab her attention. How are you holding up?"

"Getting there. We had a struggle with Ami yesterday. I walked into her bedroom, and she was packing an overnight bag. It took me nearly two hours to talk her out of going back to her parents, last night."

"I can only imagine what the pair of you are going through right now, but if Ami hadn't braved today, the case against him would have been seriously jeopardised." She fidgeted, eager to get hold of Fiona.

"That's what we told Ami last night. She seemed a little better this morning. I'm not sure how it's going in there, though. Lorne, is everything all right? You seem agitated."

"Sorry, hon. Need the loo. I'll try to get Fiona's attention. Talk soon." Lorne promptly made her way back to the courtroom entrance. She opened the door and squeezed through.

The court usher looked her over and placed a finger to his lips. She nodded and scanned the visitors' gallery for Fiona. After locating her in the second row, Lorne made her way over, all the while hearing Ami's faint voice describe the events of what happened the night she was attacked by Gibson.

Fiona eyed her with startled concern when Lorne sat on the bench next to her. "What are you doing here?" she asked in a hushed whisper.

"I need to see you outside," Lorne whispered urgently.

"But if I leave Ami now, she'll crumble."

"I wouldn't ask if it wasn't important, Fiona. Please?"

Reluctantly, Fiona stood. Lorne glanced over to the stand and smiled a reassuring smile at a panic-stricken Ami. The defence lawyer pounced on the distracted Ami, which almost made Fiona reconsider leaving the court.

Lorne grabbed Fiona's elbow and steered her out the door. "I'm sorry, Fiona. I need the keys to your flat."

"What? Lorne, you're scaring me. What's happened?"

Lorne peered in Linda's direction and saw that she and the other girl were approaching them. Hurriedly, she said, "Damn. Fiona, Blackie is dead. I need to remove his body before Ami and Linda see it. It'll crush them. Please, don't tell them. Just give me your keys."

A bewildered Fiona delved into her handbag and passed Lorne her bundle of keys. "Why? How?" As she asked the obvious questions, her confusion gave way to anger. She gasped. "He did it, didn't he?"

"I'm not sure. I think Blackie was poisoned. Please, don't react and cause Linda to worry. I'm on my way over there now with Tony. I'll get the keys back to you as soon as I can." Lorne rubbed Fiona's upper arm and left the building before Linda reached them.

Twenty minutes later, Lorne and Tony pulled up outside the girls' flat and let themselves in. Lorne ran over to Blackie and checked for any signs of life, but he felt cold to the touch. A tsunami of emotions swept through her slightly trembling body. The guilt she felt for placing the dog in such a volatile situation clawed at and squeezed her heart.

Tony had disappeared into the small kitchen and came out carrying a black bag. He shook it out and then knelt on the floor beside Lorne. He winced briefly because of his infection. He draped his arm across her shoulders, and he kissed her cheek to hurry her up.

Lorne cleaned up the blood and saliva first, and as they jointly placed Blackie in the bag, Lorne muttered, "I'm sorry, Blackie. Rest in peace, love."

They carried the dog's body out to the car and put it gently in the boot. Lorne looked around nervously, worried what the neighbours might think. Luckily, no one was around.

On the journey back to the court to drop off the keys, Lorne spoke only once. "I know exactly where I want him to be buried. Out in the paddock, underneath the tree he used to mark."

When they arrived back at the courthouse, a large group of journalists were shoving each other for the best spot as they waited for their prey on the pavement. Lorne glanced at the clock on the dashboard. Could it really be four thirty already?

"I'll be right back," she told Tony. She slammed the door and barged through the crowd. Inside, she found the three girls and Linda's friend, huddled together in their usual spot. By the entrance, Gibson and his entourage were busy prettying themselves up for the waiting press outside.

Lorne narrowed her eyes when Gibson's arrogant gaze met hers.

For the longest moment, they glared at each other before his mother tugged on his arm. "Come on, darling. She's not worth it."

Lorne bit back the retort that had settled on her lips and was dying to be released. Is your mother really that naïve? They say a mother's love knows no bounds. It sickened her to see such loyalty for a rapist and murderer. You'll get yours, rich boy!

She broke eye contact with him, scanned his Savile Row–suited body with genuine disgust, and headed towards the girls. She met Fiona halfway and returned the keys. "We've cleaned up. How are things progressing here?"

Fiona gave a brief nod, then looked over Lorne's shoulder at Gibson. "It's up to the jury, now. Not sure how long they will take to come to a verdict. I'm so proud of the way Linda and Ami coped with the annihilation of their characters. Not sure I would have survived all that crap, if I was in their shoes."

"I have a feeling the jury won't be out for long. I'll see if I can be here tomorrow. Depends on what happens with my father."

Eyeing Gibson with contempt, Fiona asked, "How is he?"

"He had a comfortable night. I'm going to visit him later; I'll know more then. What are you going to tell the girls about Blackie?"

"I was hoping you'd help me come up with an excuse."

"For now, why don't we tell them that he wasn't feeling too good, and he's come back home with me for a few days?"

"Sounds perfect, Lorne. Poor Blackie. I'm not sure I'll be able to ever have another dog. The guilt of what we put him through is just too much to bear." Fiona's eyes grew wet with threatening tears.

"Chin up. Don't let the other girls see how upset you are. I better go. Tony is parked on double yellows out front. I'll give you a ring either later on this evening or tomorrow."

They bid each other farewell, and Lorne exited the courthouse before the attention seekers did. The Gibsons soon followed, and Lorne almost got crushed in the resulting stampede.

She jumped in the passenger seat of the car and let out a huge sigh. "Get me out of here."

Tony started the engine and indicated out into the stream of late afternoon traffic and headed home.

Carol greeted them and reassured them that the place hadn't fallen down during their absence. Tony went in search of a wheelbarrow and spade. Lorne and Tony hoisted Blackie's body out of the vehicle and into the barrow. Then the three of them trudged out to Blackie's favourite tree. Tony started digging a large hole, while Lorne told Carol that the case was drawing to a conclusion.

"We'll hear the outcome tomorrow," Carol said confidently.

Out of the corner of her eye, Lorne noticed the way Carol periodically shook her head as she watched Tony dig the grave. She hoped and prayed that Carol was wrong about how the case would end, but her gut instinct was that come tomorrow she would have a lot of consoling to do.

Carol said a beautiful prayer over Blackie as Tony and Lorne lowered him into the deep hole. Lorne turned and buried her head in her husband's chest as the tears finally fell for her departed companion.

The three went into the kitchen, where Lorne insisted that Carol should join them for dinner. "It'll only be pizza, but I'd love you to join us—my way of thanking you for all you've done today, Carol."

"If you insist, who am I to argue? I wanted to have a chat about the little Yorkie I spotted in the kennels, anyway. Any chance I can offer her a new home?" Carol asked hesitantly.

Lorne smiled. "That's the dog I was telling you about. Little Nelly and you would make an excellent match. Don't you think, Tony?"

Tony nodded. "No doubts in my mind whatsoever."

"I don't want special treatment. I know you have to carry out home checks, et cetera. I'm not opposed to that."

"I'm sure there won't be a problem there, Carol."

"Now tell me all about your new business and why you decided to go it alone?"

Lorne spent the next fifteen minutes assembling the pizzas while explaining what had driven her to become a PI. Carol listened without interruption as Lorne also told her about how she'd met Tony and how he'd lost his leg in Afghanistan.

At the end, Carol sat back in her chair, looking thoughtful. "I'd love to be part of your team, Lorne."

She placed the pizzas under the grill and went back to sit opposite Carol. "In what way?"

"I just find it all so fascinating. In respect to the PIing I think you know my abilities could be helpful in solving your cases, more so now that you've left the force—no restrictions to work with, as such. Around here, I could do what I did today, stand in when needed, to give you all a break. It must be almost impossible to find reliable people to help out who would put the animal's needs before their own."

For a second or two, Lorne found that she was dumbfounded by Carol's statement. Then as the idea sunk in, she felt like jumping for joy at Carol's suggestion. "That'd be great. Wow, when everyone is fit and well, this team will be a team to be reckoned with. Can't wait to tell Dad. He's more than a little sceptical about all things paranormal. Should make for entertaining discussions at our case meetings."

They both laughed as Tony rejoined them. "Mmm... Something smells great. What's so funny, you two?"

"We'll tell you over dinner. Ham and pineapple topping for you, hon?"

During dinner, they bounced a few ideas around how the business was going to go forward. Lorne smiled at her two associates and felt a renewed vigour about being a PI again.

After dinner, they waved Carol off, then hurried over to the hospital for a quick visit. Jade had been there most of the day and was getting ready to leave when they walked into the room.

"Any change?" Lorne asked, kissing her sister on the cheek.

"They say he's improving, but I haven't witnessed any change in him yet." Jade swept her father's hair off his forehead and gently kissed him goodbye.

"We probably won't see any change for a few days. You get off. Give my love to Luigi and the boys. Thanks for sitting with Dad today."

"Any time. I know how busy you are. Sorry for being a grouch yesterday. Ring me if there's any change. I'll be here all day tomorrow, so do what you have to do back home, Lorne."

"You're a sweetheart. Actually, the jury is out on a case we're working on so I need to be there rather than at the kennels. I'll ring you soon."

The two sisters embraced, and Jade gave Tony a friendly punch on the arm as she walked past him to leave the room. Lorne hated falling out with her sister; it was good to feel forgiven by Jade.

It was the briefest of visits, as her father was still unconscious.

Lorne and Tony finally got home around nine, exhausted and ready for bed.

CHAPTER TWENTY-ONE

Somehow Lorne managed to oversleep the next morning. She was still frantically running around, feeding and exercising the dogs, when Carol arrived at eight fifteen.

"Slow down. I'll take care of the dogs. Shoo... Get ready. The girls will be expecting you."

Glancing at her watch, Lorne covered her face with her hands and then pulled her hair at the roots. "I'm never going to make it by nine."

"Take a few deep breaths, then go and jump in the shower. You'll be fine."

And she was.

Lorne pulled out of the driveway and got on the main road into London at five minutes to nine, leaving Carol and Tony to finish the chores back at home.

Storm clouds gathered on the horizon in front of her and matched the ominous and foreboding feeling that was churning up her insides. Carol's words rattled around in her mind: 'He'll get off, you know.' For the girls' sake, Lorne hoped Gibson didn't get off.

By the time Lorne parked the car and ran into the courthouse, it was almost nine thirty. The three girls were already there, looking extremely anxious, but their expressions turned to relief once they saw her. "Sorry I'm late. Hectic morning on top of an exhausting day yesterday. Hey, try not to look so petrified. The hard part is over with now."

The girls all mumbled the same thing under their breath: "Is it?"

Lorne quickly came to the conclusion that it would be best not to say anything further.

Linda inhaled sharply; Lorne followed her gaze back to the entrance. Gibson had just breezed through the door as though he didn't have a care in the world. He was wearing a crisp grey designer suit. The whiteness of his shirt showed off his recently obtained tan to the maximum.

He glanced in their direction. His eyes bore into Lorne's. For a moment, she detected a slip in his cool arrogance.

Before Lorne could assess him further, the usher of the court announced that the jury had reached their verdict and urged everyone to take their seats immediately.

Lorne turned to see the girls fiercely clutching each other. "Think positively. Let's go." Heads held high, they all walked up the corridor that had taken on a sudden chill and through the double doors into the courtroom. They sat at the end of the benches closest to the door so they could get out of there as soon as the verdict was read out.

Gibson's smile slipped as he made his way into the dock. His defence counsel were doing their best to keep his spirits high. However, his chest rose and fell heavily. When it comes to the crunch, Gibson, your cockiness is wavering now, isn't it?

She felt a sucker punch hit her solar plexus, though, when she witnessed the confidence oozing out of his counsel.

The room fell silent at the same moment a door at the far end opened and the jurors filed in. Once they were settled in their seats, the door opened behind the judge's ornate chair, and the stern-faced rotund judge joined them.

"All rise." Everyone in the room stood until the judge sat in his throne-like chair, then they all sat down. "Members of the jury, have you reached your verdict?" asked the court usher.

The spokesman on the end, nearest the jury, stood and nodded. "We have."

"What is your verdict?"

The jury spokesman, a mature man with a receding hairline, hesitated for a brief moment before he stated adamantly, "Not guilty."

Lorne closed her eyes as she heard the three girls gasp and start to sob. She quickly opened them again when she heard Gibson's elation filling the courtroom. His parents grinned broadly with relief, leading Lorne to believe that they weren't all that confident in their son's innocence to begin with.

Fiona glanced over at Lorne, a pleading in her eyes.

"Come on. Let's go. There's no point hanging around here."

Lorne and the girls hurried out of the courtroom. Lorne looked out the main doors to see the excited crowd pushing and pulling each other for the best position. "We're going to have to face them. It's either make a run for it now or wait until Gibson milks his victory. Are you three up to this?"

Three nods came her way. Lorne grabbed Ami's hand and rushed through the doors, they were immediately pounced on by a reporter she knew well. "Ms Simpkins, how do you feel about today's verdict?"

Lorne ignored the question, but after it was followed by several similar ones, she heard a voice behind her shout out, "Gibson might have been found not guilty in there, but he knows he's guilty of not one, but three heinous crimes. He'll get what's coming to him!"

Fiona lifted her head, and with a sobbing Linda clinging to her arm, she stormed past Lorne and ran down the remaining steps. Thankfully, the crowd remained in place, waiting for the victorious defendant.

"You really shouldn't have said that, Fiona," Lorne reprimanded as they dashed along the street to the car park.

"I know, but I just couldn't hold back any longer. They ask such dumb questions. Anyway, it's true." Fiona chewed her bottom lip as if she wanted to take back the threat.

"Meaning?" Lorne demanded, an uneasy feeling tugging at her gut.

Fiona's face reddened, and her expression darkened. "I won't let him get away with this, Lorne."

"You can't go taking things into your own hands. Why should you end up in prison? Two wrongs will never make a right."

"I know that, Lorne." Fiona had the decency to look ashamed for a second or two before the injustice of the situation sunk in, and hatred darkened her features once more. "I've said too much. The less you know, the better."

"What? You can't be serious? I won't let you do this. I demand to know what you're planning to do?"

But Lorne was already speaking to the girls' backs as they broke away from her and hurriedly made their way to their car. Damn!

She turned to face the courtroom again, contemplating what she should do next, when the arrogant Gibson, his arms raised and fists clenched in victory, appeared at the top of the steps. After their initial enthusiasm, the crowd's shouting died down.

Lorne walked back to listen to what he had to say.

"My name has been dragged through the mud. My reputation is now in tatters because of these false allegations. I'm delighted that the jury saw through the three girls' lies. They have conspired against me in the hope that telling the same unbelievable stories, I would be thrown behind bars. Maybe they've watched too many crime or forensic shows on TV and believed they had thought of the perfect crime to stitch me up. Anyway, I'm glad the jury saw through their scam and had the sense to show me their support. I'm an innocent bystander in this crime; they're the criminals for the lies they've told and the damage they've caused my, until now, unblemished reputation."

You jumped up little... Maybe the girls would be justified if they went it alone. Men like him deserved to be pulled down a peg or two.

Thinking she couldn't listen to his lies anymore, Lorne made her way back to the car. On the way, she rang Katy. "Hiya. It's me. The bastard got off with it."

"Shit! Bet that didn't go down well with the girls."

"Nope. I have a funny feeling they're going to try to mete out their own justice."

Katy tutted and released a heavy breath. "I hope you tried to dissuade them, Lorne?"

"Of course I did, but the look in Fiona's eyes was enough to tell me to butt out. I'll let them calm down for a day or two and then get in touch with them. I'll try to talk them out of what they have planned."

"Very wise. Give me a call if you need backup at all. Gotta fly, I've got to interview a suspect."

Lorne hung up and started the engine. She drove home on autopilot again, something she seemed to be doing more and more those days, her mind lingering on the day's events and what the girls' plans likely were.

Tony was in the courtyard waiting for her. He opened the car and kissed her on the lips when she got out. "Not good news, I take it."

"How can a guy like that twist the jury around his finger? What's wrong with people? Why can't they see when they're being played?"

Tony placed an arm around her shoulder and pulled her head against his chest. "We'll get him, Lorne."

"We better do it quick, before the girls beat us to it," she stated, pulling away from him. "It might have been a spur-of-the-moment comment, but Fiona threatened they were going to get revenge."

Tony shook his head. "Great! You're talking vigilante style?"

Lorne shrugged and threw her arms out to the side and walked towards the back door. "Who knows?"

Carol was standing by the kettle and flicked the switch when Lorne and Tony came through the door. "He got off, then?"

"As you predicted, Carol. The justice system is so screwed up at the moment."

"Hmm... You can see why some folks are intent on taking the law into their own hands."

"What makes you say that, Carol?" Lorne asked, wondering if she'd had one of her visions.

Carol hitched up her left shoulder. "Not sure, really. Maybe something I read in the newspaper the other day sparked a memory. I'm sure the girls wouldn't do anything like that."

The more Lorne thought about it, the more her apprehension grew, until curiosity finally got the better of her.

Directly after lunch was finished, she rang Fiona. The young woman was a little offhand with her, not what Lorne had expected at all. She found it tough to raise the subject about wanting retribution and danced around it. Finally, she had ended the call, telling Fiona that she was only a phone call away and that if either of them needed her help in the future, she'd drop everything to help them.

During the following two days, Lorne thoroughly cleaned the house and kennels. It got rid of the frustrations, but the sense of failure and disgust remained. By the time Lorne's father was released from hospital, her feelings had dissipated to little more than a niggling annoyance.

As she settled her father into his bed, he patted the cover, insisting she sit with him.

She sat. "What's up, Dad?"

He reached out, clutched her hand, and placed it lovingly against his pyjama-clad chest. "I was about to ask the same thing, love."

"I'm fine, Dad. I'm concerned about you, that's all." Lorne's head dipped.

Her father lifted her chin with a finger, forcing her to look him in the eye. "That's part of it. Lorne, I know the case didn't turn out as planned, but I won't allow you to blame yourself for that," he said softly.

She smiled a reassuring smile. "Even when you're desperately ill, you're still the most perceptive man I know. Rest, now. I'll bring you in a cuppa in a while." She handed him the latest Karen Rose novel, and he grinned.

"Everything will work out for the best, you'll see."

Lorne kissed his forehead and left the room, contemplating his words as she made her way back to the kitchen where Tony was waiting for her.

"Why the sad face, hon?"

"I'm not sad, Tony. Just distracted."

He walked towards her, threw his arms over her shoulders and pulled her to him. "You think and worry too much."

He was right. It would be impossible to switch off a niggling doubt just like that, though.

CHAPTER TWENTY-TWO

Several weeks later, Fiona was scan-reading a new account, ready for an opening meeting with the client, when her office phone rang. "Hello?"

"He's here. Shit, what do I do?"

"Linda, who's there? What are you talking about?" Fiona stared ahead at the large picture of a black rose that adorned her small office wall.

Her sister's heavy breathing surged down the line. "Gibson."

That hated name grabbed Fiona's full attention. "Don't panic. Is anyone there with you?"

"Yes, my boss. Oh, Fiona, he keeps looking over and smirking at me."

"Okay, you know what we discussed. We knew there was a possibility he'd show up there, hon. I'm sure he won't do anything while someone else is around. What does he want?"

"Christ, my skin is crawling. He's after a new house. Of all the estate agents in this road, let alone this city, he chooses to come in here and badger me."

Fiona's brain clicked into gear. This might be the opportunity they'd been waiting for. It was time to put their plan into action. "Don't let it show how scared you are of him. Smile as though you're fine with what happened and that you've forgiven him."

"What? Are you insane?" Linda whispered harshly.

"Just do it. We'll talk later."

Reluctantly Linda agreed before hanging up. For the next ten minutes, Fiona jotted down notes that had nothing to do with the clients she had to meet that morning. She scribbled away frantically until a knock on the door startled her.

"Ready?" her boss poked his head in the office. His smile dropped when she looked up at him. "Anything wrong?"

Fiona hastily gathered her plans and tucked them into the drawer of her desk. "Nothing. Just making some final adjustments. Be with you in two minutes; need to powder my nose first."

Her boss shook his head, unconvinced by her words.

She nipped to the loo to replenish her lipstick and pulled a comb through her hair. As she studied her reflection in the mirror, she wondered if she could ever go through with the plan she'd hatched. Narrowing her eyes, she conjured up Gibson's smug face and knew instantly that the decision was a no-brainer. She forced his image from her mind again to concentrate on the large contract she had to try to obtain in the upcoming meeting.

After several hours of strained negotiations with her boss by her side, Fiona breathed a sigh of relief when she left the boardroom with the signed contract in her sweaty palm and the promise of a hefty bonus winging its way to her bank account. On the journey home, her business day complete, she pondered how she was going to broach the subject of revenge with the girls and wondered if they would have enough courage to carry out the plan.

Letting herself in to the communal hallway outside their flat, her gaze rose to the ceiling when she heard her sister's shrill voice retelling the day's events. She opened the flat door to find a distraught Ami listening and trying to comfort Linda.

Fiona plonked herself down on the sofa and wrapped an arm around her sister's shuddering shoulders. "Listen, Linda, I've put up with this for months now. I cannot and will not put up with it any longer."

Linda spun round to look at her. She frowned. "I'm sorry I'm such a burden to you, Fi—"

"My God, is that what you seriously think?" Fiona shot back in disbelief. "Oh, I see. You think I was having a go at you. Nothing could be further from the truth! I meant I think it's time to put an end to this guy torturing you—both of you—and this is how we're going to do it."

For the next half hour, Fiona explained the proposal that had preoccupied her mind at work for most of the day. At times, Linda and Ami stared at her open-mouthed, but as Fiona reached the end of her speech the pair nodded and rubbed their hands together in glee.

All they had to do was wait patiently for the appropriate time to present itself.

CHAPTER TWENTY-THREE

The girls didn't have to wait long for the opportune moment to arrive.

Two days later, Gibson entered the estate agent's office where Linda worked. Again he dealt with her boss. Linda had reassured her boss that she was over what had happened and that she would be the ultimate professional when dealing with Gibson. With the extortionate amount of disposable income he was willing to invest in the 'right property,' Gibson was being treated as a very special client. Linda knew that if she showed any distaste or hatred towards him, he would probably take his business elsewhere, and the blame would lie at her door, jeopardising her future career.

Linda was busy updating the pictures to a few of the properties they'd had on their books for a while.

Tim, her boss, called over, "Linda. Any chance you can show Mr. Gibson around this property in Mayfair this afternoon?"

Before looking up, Linda gulped and tried to compose herself. The last thing she wanted to do was let him know how much he still scared and intimidated her.

With her sister's well thought out plan at the forefront of her mind, she beamed at the two men. "I'd be delighted. What time did you have in mind, Mr. Gibson?" Just saying his name caused an unwanted shudder to ripple up her spine.

Gibson placed a contemplating finger on his cheek. "How about five? Is that all right with you and the vendors?"

Tim intervened. "No problem there. The house is empty, as the vendors had to move back to Texas last month. All right with you, Linda?"

She cleared her throat to dislodge the lump that had developed. "I'll meet you there at five on the dot." She gave Gibson the sweetest, most charming smile she could muster.

When Gibson left the office, Tim approached her desk. "Are you sure that you're all right with this, Linda? I feel awful, putting you in such a position. The thing is, Gibson wouldn't deal with anyone else. Maybe he wants to make amends in some way."

"To be honest, Tim, I'm a little apprehensive about meeting the guy alone, but I appreciate how valuable his business is." She winked at her thirty-year-old boss and added, "Maybe there could be an extra bonus in the sale for me, too. What do you reckon?"

He turned and laughed all the way back to his desk. "Forever the trier, aren't you? We'll see."

Linda picked up her handbag and checked that her mobile was inside before she made her way out to the tiny kitchenette area at the rear of the agency, where the staff prepared their drinks and ate lunch. She placed a call to Fiona.

"Everything all right, Linda?"

"Umm... Couldn't be better, Sis. Any chance you can sort out some time off this afternoon?"

"Let me check the diary. I have a brief meeting at three thirty. What time was you thinking of and why?"

"I need you to be at a certain address by five o'clock," Linda told her as an unexpected bout of excitement shot through her.

Her sister sighed. "Depends where it is, love. You're being awfully secretive."

Linda gave Fiona the address. She heard her sister tear a sheet of paper from her notebook and waited for her to scribble down the information. Then Linda announced breathlessly, "It's time to put our plan into action."

"You're kidding? Seriously? Today? Are you okay with this?"

Linda chuckled. "At least give me a chance to answer a question before you ask the next one. I'm soooo ready for this. The idiot's arrogance was on show again today when he made the appointment. I can't wait to knock that smug look off his supercilious tanned face."

"Me, neither. Are you going to ring Ami?"

"Just about to do it now. Wait outside the property; there's a park across the road from the house. I'll give you the heads-up from the front bedroom on the first floor. God, I hope we can pull this off, Fi."

"Positive mental attitude, sweetie. Between us, we'll make this happen. We'll wait for your signal. Tell Ami I'll be waiting in the park for her. Good luck, and Linda..."

"Yes, Fi?"

"Be brave and confident that we have your back."

Linda smiled, and her eyes misted up. "Love you. See you later."

She hung up and left a voicemail message on Ami's phone. Linda noted the time on her watch and realised that Ami was probably held up in a lecture. She knew Ami would get back to her the minute her schedule allowed her to.

Linda boiled the kettle and poured two instant coffees for her and Tim and returned to the office.

"Wondered where you had disappeared to. I'm gasping for a drink, good call. Have you finished updating those files yet? I'd like to get them up on the website this afternoon if at all possible."

She handed him his mug and nodded. "Almost finished; another five minutes should do it. I'll pass them over as soon as I'm done."

She sat at her desk and put all thoughts of Gibson out of her mind and got on with the task her boss had set her.

Within minutes, she had handed him the completed files and was just about to start on the next thing on her to-do list when her mobile jangled that she had a text. She opened the message to see the words 'I'll be there. Revenge will be sweet.'

Linda smiled as she deleted Ami's message. A sense of pride filled her, and she puffed out her chest. What better friends and family could one hope to have?

The rest of the day was full of deepening trepidation. Gibson's handsome but arrogant features constantly flooded her overworked mind. Silly reasons why she should pull out of the meeting with Gibson knocked against her skull on several occasions, but she quickly dismissed them.

When the clock on the wall above her boss's head reached four o'clock, that meant she had exactly half an hour left before she had to leave for her rendezvous. Those final thirty minutes were some of the longest of her life, coming a close second to the time when Gibson had raped her. All the pain and fear she had suffered that night ripped through her.

Her determination grew tenfold. If she had any doubts before that they were doing the right thing, those doubts were now being pushed to the huge abyss in the back of her mind.

Five minutes to go before her departure time, Linda gathered the details of the property she was going to see and to several other houses in the same area. She had decided to tell her boss that she would go straight home after showing Gibson round the property he was interested in and the similar ones she had picked out a few streets away from it. It would give her the excuse she needed for her extended leave from the office. There was no telling how long Fiona's plan would take to fulfill, once they got started.

Linda looked up again as the minute hand agonisingly moved to half past four. After drawing in a sharp breath and releasing it, she rose from her desk, gathered the keys and the details to all the properties she intended to visit—at least, as far as her boss was concerned—and said farewell to her boss for the evening.

Her legs trembled, and it felt as if her shoes were suddenly made of lead as she made her way out the back of her office to the car park at the rear.

Normally Linda was an error-free driver, but during the journey, she repeatedly missed gears and even ran a red light. Pull yourself together, girl.

When she pulled into Drake's Avenue, she parked in a free space at the top of the road. There, she had a moment's hesitation as to whether she and the girls were doing the right thing. But images of that degrading night drifted into her mind once again.

She restarted the engine and slowly made her way down the road. She parked her car outside the Georgian mansion house at two minutes to the hour.

Glancing around, she couldn't see Gibson's Ferrari anywhere. Linda let herself in the front door of the house and immediately ran upstairs to the front bedroom. A flash of red in the park across the street caught her eye. Is that the girls?

The front door bell chimed.

Panic shot through her faster than a lightning bolt. She ran back down the stairs, almost tripping on the final step. Remember: Stay calm at all times.

She planted a huge smile on her lightly made-up face and opened the door wide. "Hello, Mr. Gibson. It's lovely to see you again. Do come in."

Her words appeared to catch him off-guard. At first he looked bewildered, but then he smiled graciously and entered the house. Linda discreetly lifted the catch on the front door and swiftly shut it behind him. Her heart rate began to escalate, and there was little she could do to control it except take several steadying breaths.

Linda led the way around the lower floor highlighting the properties good points. Gibson was unusually quiet, almost reflective, and she couldn't help wondering if he regretted what he'd done to her.

The rooms were empty apart from the odd pieces of furniture that had seen better days and had been deliberately left behind by the previous owner.

She did, however, get a wow out of him the second he walked into the enormous kitchen. The flecks in the granite worktops twinkled in the late afternoon sunlight as it danced across the surface.

"If you'd like to follow me upstairs." She cringed inwardly as she said the words she'd been dreading saying because of what it could imply. She could feel his eyes burning into the flesh of her backside as she climbed the stairs in front of him. She did her best to wiggle less, but fighting the natural movement of her body was pointless. His breathing increased as if the view was turning him on. Crap! Be calm and brave.

Once they had reached the top of the large sweeping staircase, Linda headed into the master en-suite. She crossed the oak floorboards and stood in the centre of the big bay window, looking back at Gibson, who had remained in the doorway.

He nodded his approval at the dimensions of the room.

She moved across the room to open the large fitted wardrobes, which showed off the room's adequate storage, then she pointed at the door to the en-suite, inviting him to venture in and take a look at the Victorian claw-footed bath and marbled surroundings.

His impressed expression when he rejoined her ordinarily would have sparked the pound signs to register before her eyes, knowing that a sale was imminent. But with Gibson, she took his enthusiasm with a pinch of salt. She had a feeling his enthusiasm was riddled with pretence and probably wouldn't lead anywhere.

She led the way into the double bedroom at the rear of the property. Gibson raised a questioning eyebrow at the red flock wallpaper adorning all four walls.

Linda had to admit the room did have a feel similar to a tart's boudoir. She shrugged. "The lady of the house liked to experiment with colours."

He took several steps toward her, gave her one of his devastating smiles and said, "Tell me, Linda—do you like to experiment too?"

Unknowingly she stepped back. The emphasis he'd put on the word experiment sent shockwaves of panic shooting out to every frazzled nerve ending. She had to get out of there, away from him, quickly.

Linda forced her shoulders back and squeezed past him. Her breasts touched his chest, and he attempted to grab her shoulders, but she was too quick for him. She darted for the stairs and ran down them before he had a chance to reach for her again.

Linda sprinted into the lounge and waited for Gibson to follow her.

Gibson screeched to a halt when he saw Linda standing alongside her sister. He turned sharply when he heard a sound behind him and tried to duck when he saw the baseball bat aimed at his head, but Ami made a direct hit. Gibson crumpled to the floor, knocked out cold.

CHAPTER TWENTY-FOUR

"Jesus! What do we do now, Fi?" Linda asked as the three of them gripped each other's forearms and stared at the prostrate figure beneath them.

Fiona took charge, she glanced around the room and pointed. "Ami, get that chair. Linda, there's a rope in the carrier bag in the corner."

Linda and Ami ran to different sides of the room and returned with the items. Fiona positioned the old wooden dining chair at the rear of Gibson and knelt down beside him. "Help me get him into the chair," Fiona demanded urgently.

Between the three of them, they heaved Gibson's dead weight into the chair amidst plenty of heavy breathing and straining noises. Fiona put her Girl Guide's experience to use; she quickly and expertly tied Gibson's wrists behind him to the wooden upright of the chair. Standing back, she admired her work.

After a final tug on the rope, she turned to Linda and Ami. "If anyone has any second thoughts about this, speak up now?"

One look at the girl's faces gave Fiona her answer. "Linda, is there a cup or pot left in the kitchen cupboard?"

"Not sure. Why?"

"Will you go look for me, please? If you find anything suitable, fill it with water."

Linda left the room and came back to find Fiona delving into the carrier bag. One by one Fiona laid the contents of the bag on the floorboards in front of her: a hacksaw, pliers, matches, and a newspaper. She arranged the items carefully on the wooden floor.

Linda and Ami looked on in astonishment. They had never discussed what would happen to Gibson once he'd been caught. When the girls glanced up at Fiona, she had an evil glint in her eye, and an ominous smirk tugged at her red lipstick–stained lips.

Fiona held out her hand for the glass of water. Linda hesitated for a moment or two, then reluctantly passed the glass to her sister. She threw the water, hard, in Gibson's face. He coughed and spluttered into life again.

Immediately, his gaze narrowed at the three of them. "What the fuck is this all about?"

Fiona noticed Linda cower back from his anger-filled tone. Fiona looked her way and winked, and instantly Linda stood proud and tall again, ready for the fight that lay ahead of them.

Gibson warily watched the exchange between the girls before he verbally attacked them, "When I get out of here, I'm going straight to the police. You do know that kidnapping is a crime, don't you?"

His gaze homed in on Linda. Fiona suspected that he thought it wouldn't take much to unnerve her. Fiona took up the verbal challenge. "Oh, right! So you don't reckon rape is a crime, then?"

Gibson's mouth turned up in a sneer. "In case you need reminding, I was found not guilty by a court of law."

"Yeah, and we all know why, don't we? Money talks."

Gibson snorted. "The jury recognised that I was the one telling the truth. That's why I got off. These two were begging me for it."

Fiona heard Linda's breathing become more pronounced and saw her stiffen with anger. Defending her sister's honour, she stepped towards Gibson and backhanded him hard across his face. "Bastard! I'd watch your mouth, if I were you." Fiona glanced pointedly down at the tools in front of her.

Gibson shook his head and twisted his jaw from side to side. A trickle of blood ran down the side of his mouth from where Fiona's hand had made contact. "You wouldn't dare."

"Big mistake, buster." Fiona reached down and picked up the pliers. She turned to Ami and Linda. "Grab his right arm."

Both of the girls pounced on Gibson. Ami held the lower part of his arm near the wrist, while Linda grasped his upper arm. They held it tight as Fiona approached the struggling hostage.

He cried out, all his bravado forgotten as Fiona pulled the thumbnail from his right hand. "Jesus, no! Don't touch me! Ahhhhh!"

"That's just the beginning, Gibson. We demand an apology." Fiona searched in her handbag and pulled out a mini tape recorder. She pressed the Record button.

Gibson seized his opportunity. "Help! They have me tied up. They're torturing me to get an admission of guilt. Anything I say will be said under duress."

Fiona ripped another nail off the same hand and his scream filled the room.

Fiona was lost in a manic haze and at first didn't feel her sister yanking on her arm pleading with her to stop, as she delighted in the sight of the pool of blood trickling down and settling on the floorboards behind Gibson's chair.

"Fiona, please. Don't do any more."

Fiona narrowed her gaze and pulled her arm out of her sister's grasp. She leaned down and whispered in Gibson's ear, "It's only going to get worse. Admit that you lied now, or there will be no turning back. This is your final chance."

Gibson shook his head adamantly. "Never! You haven't got the balls to go through with this," he added naïvely.

"Really? And just how attached are you to your balls, Gibson?" Fiona snarled, her gaze dropping down to his crotch.

Her words hung in the air for several seconds before Linda said, "Fiona, please don't do it."

Fiona turned on her sister. "After what he did to you, how could you possibly stick up for him?" Linda reeled at the viciousness in Fiona's voice. Am I taking this too far?

"He's not worth it, Fi. You can see how stubborn he is. He's never going to admit to raping either Ami or me. Please rethink what you're doing."

Fiona shook her head from side to side in defiance, slowly and deliberately—almost tauntingly. "There's no turning back now, Sis."

"Listen to your sister, you dumb bitch. Let me go now, and I won't press charges against you," Gibson shouted.

With her face inches from his, Fiona sneered. "You won't get the chance to press charges, smartarse. By the time I've finished with you, you'll be a quivering wreck—an ugly one, at that. No one will take any notice of you. You'll be a nobody."

The room fell silent. The only noise that could be heard was Gibson swallowing.

Fiona reached down and picked up the hacksaw. Gibson's eyes nearly popped out of his head. Unconcerned Fiona walked behind the chair.

Gibson's head turned swiftly to follow her. Disbelief written all over his face. Fiona gripped the little finger on the hand that had escaped pain thus far. His screams rebounded off the inanimate walls as the blade slowly sliced through the flesh and bone.

Fiona heard her sister gag and spit on the floor. "Please, Fi. I'm begging you to stop it!"

But Linda's pitiful pleading only enraged Fiona more and spurred her on. *How could she beg me not to hurt him after all he's done to her?*

Fiona took hold of Gibson's little finger, and despite his futile attempt to dislodge his finger from her grasp, she hacked away just below the joint, severing it in half.

* * *

"I'll get it!" Lorne shouted when she heard the phone ringing in the lounge. After six impatient rings, she finally answered it. "Hello?"

"Thank God! I thought you were out."

"Carol, is that you?" Lorne asked, trying to catch her breath.

"Lorne, oh Lord! We have trouble. I can see this ending badly."

"Whoa, hold on a minute. What are you talking about?" Lorne looked up to see a worried Tony lean his head against the doorframe, a quizzical expression on his face. She shrugged her left shoulder slightly in response and turned her attention back to the psychic.

"We need to act quickly, before it's too late. The girls are out of control—"

"Right now, Carol, I need you to tell me what you mean. I haven't got a clue what the heck you're talking about."

"Can you and Tony come and pick me up?"

Lorne blew a heavy breath out in exasperation. "We can't both come. There's Dad to consider. Just tell me what you've seen or felt?"

"The three girls have that Gibson fellow. Lorne, they're doing dreadful things to him. If we don't try and stop them soon, I fear it's going to be too late."

"Shit! Any idea where?"

"We don't have time for this, dear. Get over here immediately."

"I'll be there in fifteen minutes. Hold tight, Carol." Lorne hung up and rushed past Tony.

He gently grabbed her arm. "What is it?"

"I have to get over to Carol's right away. Gibson is in danger."

"You're not making any sense, love."

"Carol's had one of her visions, and the girls are holding Gibson captive and doing terrible things to him, apparently. I need to pick Carol up. Will you be all right here with Dad?"

"Go. Although if I was in your shoes, I wouldn't rush to save that scumbag. Let the girls have their fun with him."

Lorne smirked but shook her head. "You're a wicked man, Tony Warner. You know I can't stand by and let something like that happen, even if I wanted to cheer the girls on. I'll give you a ring later."

He pulled her into his arms and kissed her hard on the lips. "Be careful out there."

"I intend to be."

CHAPTER TWENTY-FIVE

As Lorne turned into Carol Lang's road, she spotted the woman standing by the curb, anxiously pacing up and down in front of her tiny terraced house.

"What took you so long? You've been half an hour or more," Carol said, falling into the passenger seat.

"Damn rush hour traffic. I'm here now. Have you seen anything else?"

Carol's hands went to either side of her temples, and she squeezed her eyes tightly shut. "They have him tied to a chair. I'm seeing a green area opposite the house. Is one of the girls an estate agent?"

Impressed, Lorne replied, "I believe Linda is, yes. Why?"

"They laid a trap for him, and he walked right into it. What's the term—"

"Jesus, I think you're thinking of a honey trap. I'm not sure it could be called that, but I get your drift." Lorne knew the girls had been destroyed by the verdict, but she wouldn't have thought it possible for them to do something as despicable as this. A scorned woman was someone not to tackle lightly. Two scorned women were a force to be reckoned with, while three scorned women would and could be downright dangerous, as Gibson was finding out. "Any idea where they are? Can you see what type of house, Carol?"

She gave a defeated shrug and ran a frustrated hand through her hair. "I'm not getting an image of the house yet, only the green space near it."

"Great! There are tons of green spaces in London and on the outskirts too. Anything else?"

"All I can see are the three girls surrounding Gibson. The room appears to be empty of all other furniture. Let me look deeper," Carol told her before she fell silent again.

Lorne scanned all around her as she thought of possible areas they could try that were relatively close by. With the darkness descending around them, she knew it was imperative to get moving soon. She glanced back at Carol hoping for further details.

"The house is huge. Empty and huge. Hang on—the green space is a park. It's opposite the house. Let me see if I can go outside."

Carol drifted off again. Lorne studied her closely and saw her begin to squirm in her seat. *What the heck is she doing?*

As if hearing her or reading her mind, Carol explained, "I'm walking out through the front door. It looks like a large Georgian mansion. Wait, I can see the edge of the road sign—something Gardens."

With no Sat Nav in her father's car, Lorne reached in the glove compartment and got out the London street map. It took her a while to find anything remotely similar to what Carol had described. Two possibilities immediately caught her attention. She indicated the two spots on the map with a pen and handed it to Carol. "Either of those locations look familiar?"

Silence filled the car, then Carol tapped the map with her forefinger. "I'm leaning more towards this location, Lorne. How far are we from it?"

She quickly worked out a route and then folded the map back on itself. Leaving the route she was going to take uppermost, she handed it to Carol. "I'm guessing it's a good twenty minutes from here—providing the traffic isn't too bad, that is." Lorne started the car and drove off.

"Shame you don't have one of those little blue lights attached to the roof." Carol let out a large sigh. "I fear it's going to be too late."

The words hung menacingly in the air between them. Unusually Lorne drove like a professional, possibly due to the urgency of the situation. As she drove, her mind raced at a hundred miles an hour.

With one hand gripping the steering wheel, she delved into her jacket pocket, located her mobile and punched number three on the pad. "Katy, I need a favour."

"Of course. What is it?" Katy replied, thankfully without pausing.

Lorne ran through the sketchy details they had about Gibson's possible abduction, because it had yet to be proven, and asked if it would be possible to get a patrol car to search the area.

"There's no need, I'll do better than that, Lorne." She lowered her voice. "I'm just leaving for the day, anyway. I'll take a detour and meet you at the location."

Shocked, she replied, "Katy, I can't ask you to get involved in this, it could jeopardise your career."

"Nonsense. See you there."

Katy hung up before Lorne could argue further.

A thrill ran through Lorne. It was good to be working with Katy again.

* * *

"What have you done?" Linda cried out.

Fiona looked at her frantic sister's tear-stained face and stammered, "I don't know. I never meant to go that far." She sunk to her knees beside Gibson's limp body and buried her head in her hands.

Rocking back and forth, she had to fight back the urge to throw up. She truly hadn't meant to take things quite that far, never intended to end the rapist's life like she had. But once she'd seen the suffering on his face, an uncanny evilness had taken over and driven her on. An unknown rage had guided each action using the different implements—a rage that, once it begun, had been unstoppable.

Ami tried to help Fiona to her feet. "We have to get out of here, now."

Linda shook her head. "What? We can't leave him here. I have the keys, remember. I was the last one to see him alive. There are records to prove that back at the office."

Ami asked quietly, "What will we do then? Dispose of the body?" Both Linda and Fiona's heads snapped round to look at her. "Well, what other option do we have?"

Fiona rose from the floor, and her legs almost gave way again. She leaned against the wall for support. "We need to think this through."

"I thought we had already," Linda retorted. "You're the one who went over the top, Fi. Make him suffer, you said. You didn't tell us your plan included killing him."

Fiona widened her eyes at the accusation. "I didn't have plans to kill him. What do you take me for, Linda?"

"After that little display I'm beginning to wonder if I know you at all."

Ami stepped between them, placed her hands over her ears, and shouted, "Stop it! Stop the arguing. What good will it do? What's done is done. What we need to think about is what the fuck we're going to do with the body. It's getting dark. Now would be an ideal opportunity to get rid of it—of him."

Fiona sucked in a shuddering breath. Ami was right. It was the perfect time to get rid of Gibson, once and for all. "Is there a rug in any of the rooms, Linda?"

"I'm not sure. I'll go and check." Linda ran out of the room.

Fiona could hear her footsteps above as she went from one room to another. The look of disgust on Ami's face tugged at Fiona's heart. Needing reassurance that Ami didn't hate her, she said, "I didn't mean to kill him, Ami. I couldn't stop myself. Images of him raping the pair of you... And what he did to Blackie..."

"What? Are you telling me he killed Blackie?" Ami asked before her mouth fell open.

Fiona could have kicked herself for her stupid slip of the tongue. "Lorne and I were desperate to keep that from you and Linda."

Anger replaced Ami's shock. "You don't have to explain, Fiona. Despite what he's done, he didn't deserve to die. You scared me. It was as if you had become possessed by the devil. He didn't deserve that, Fi. However much a bastard he was, he didn't deserve to die," she stated, her voice quivering.

"I know. I'll have to live with that guilt for the rest of my life. What I won't be able to live with is your and Linda's unwillingness to forgive me."

Before Ami could respond, Linda came bounding into the room. Breathlessly she told them, "In the back bedroom there's a rug. Can one of you help me bring it down?"

Ami left the room before Fiona answered. Linda ran after her, leaving Fiona alone with Gibson's tortured body and the unsatisfactory feeling that she'd damaged not one, but two relationships, because of her over-the-top actions.

Still, she couldn't worry about that now. She had to come up with an idea where to dump the body. A passing thought told her that it would be best to cut Gibson to pieces and scatter his remains around London, but she knew she wouldn't have the stomach or courage to do that.

When the girls returned carrying an eight-foot rug, Fiona untied Gibson's hands. His body immediately slumped forward and toppled off the chair onto the floor. The girls screamed before Fiona ordered them to be quiet. "Help me get him on the rug."

The three of them, positioned Gibson's body at one end and rolled the rug towards the other end.

Fiona handed Ami her car keys. "Bring the car to the front of the house and open the boot. As soon as you pull up, we'll bring him out."

Ami left the room.

Linda asked, "What are we going to do with him?"

"I've been trying to think of somewhere we can dump the body. The last thing we want is someone to discover it. Any ideas? What about an empty house out in the country or something? Do you have anything like that on your books?"

Linda contemplated the question for several seconds before she clicked her fingers together. "I've got it. Last week, we were instructed to sell a vacant farm. The family put it on the books at an extortionate price. I doubt they'll be selling it any time soon. It comes with six hundred acres of land. What if we bury him there?"

"That's a great idea. Is it very far?" Fiona tried to remember if she had a shovel in the back of her car. Her father had told her years ago to always carry one in case she had the misfortune to get snowed in anywhere.

"On the outskirts of the city. About twenty to twenty-five minutes, I suppose."

"Perfect. I think I have a shovel in the car. We could take it in turns digging, if you're up to it?"

A car door slammed.

Linda went over to the window. "Here's Ami now."

"Right. Grab that end. Oh, and sis—I love you, and I'm sorry." Fiona's eyes welled up with tears.

"I know you do, Fiona. We'll get through this together. Come on."

They heaved the rug off the floor and struggled through the house to the front door. Ami supported the rug in the middle. It took several attempts to wedge the body into the medium-sized boot, but finally Gibson's body was tucked up and secure.

CHAPTER TWENTY-SIX

Lorne pulled the car into the curb and put her hazard lights on. "Anything, Katy?"

"Nothing, as far as I can see. How far away are you?"

"I estimate about two or three minutes. Wait outside for me."

"Will do. I'll take a quick look round the back—see if I can find anything round there, first. See you soon."

Lorne hung up. "Not sure whether we have the right location or not. Katy's there now, and all is quiet. We'll take a look ourselves and then decide what to do next."

Carol nodded and seemed to go off into one of her meditative zones.

A few minutes later, Lorne drew up outside the Georgian mansion with the for sale sign outside. "Do you want to come, see if you can pick up any vibes or anything?"

"I'll do my best."

The second they got out of the car, Katy, carrying a torch, came around the corner to meet them. She greeted Lorne with a smile and a slight shrug. "Can't see a thing round the back."

Carol breezed past Lorne and Katy in a daze. She peered through the window at the front of the house and called out, "Here. They were here."

Both Lorne and Katy rushed to her side and looked through the paned window at the empty room beyond. Well, almost empty. "How can you tell, Carol?"

She pointed at the chair in the middle of the room. "In my vision, that's where Gibson was tied up."

"Really? If that's the case, where is he now?" Lorne asked mystified.

"I have no idea. Everything comes to an abrupt halt at this house," Carol said sadly.

"Please try, Carol. It's important we find them."

Katy tried the front door. It was locked. "How should we play it? Should I call it in? Without proof of a body, I'll be a laughing stock if nothing is found at the scene."

"I understand, Katy. Let's see if we can gain access to the house first, and then go from there."

They split up and tried the windows without success.

In the end, curiosity outweighed their sense of right and wrong. Katy picked up a small rock she'd found lying amongst the roses in the front garden. She tapped at the corner of the window with a pointed edge of the stone, and the windowpane shattered.

Lorne took her coat off and bashed at the glass, then she put her hand through and felt around for the window catch. She released it, and they hoisted the sash-window up.

Lorne turned to Carol. "Stay here and keep lookout. Call us if anyone comes."

"Be careful," Carol warned as first Katy then Lorne went through the opening.

Katy turned on her torch and scanned the room as the pair of them walked over to the chair. The beam from the torch highlighted the blood pooling on the floorboards behind the chair. Lorne saw something else glisten to the side of the blood and pointed to the spot she wanted Katy to shine the light.

"Is that vomit?" Katy asked, screwing her nose up.

"Looks like it—or a small amount of bile, at least. I think we have the right location. The question is, what do we do about it?"

"Have you tried contacting the girls?"

Lorne nodded. "No reply. All calls go directly to voicemail."

"Okay, what about if you call their bluff? Tell them you know what's happened and urge them to do the right thing?"

Lorne pulled her mobile out of her pocket and dialled Fiona's number. It immediately went into voicemail. Lorne spoke calmly, "Fiona, it's Lorne. We know what you've done. Ring me ASAP to discuss the issue." Her mouth twisted as she hung up. "Not sure that's going to help any. What do you think about taking a ride out to the girls' flat?"

"Fine by me," Katy replied, already turning to leave the house.

"Katy, what about this?" Lorne pointed back into the room.

"Let's see what the girls have to say and then decide. If I had my way, I'd be willing to brush this incident under the carpet. As far as I'm concerned, he got what was coming to him—if he's dead."

Lorne attributed Katy's coldness to her own unscrupulous ex-boyfriend who had constantly knocked seven bells out of her. Brushing the idea aside was something that had crossed Lorne's mind; she just hadn't had the nerve to voice her opinion out loud.

The more she thought about it, the more the idea appealed to her. At the end of the day, the only people who knew about this incident were people she knew and felt she could trust.

The three of them drove to the girls' flat. Carol stayed in Lorne's car while Lorne and Katy walked down the street to the girls' flat, which unsurprisingly was in darkness. "My guess is that no one is home," Katy said.

"Hmm… You could be right there. We'll give it a try anyway."

Their first observation proved to be correct. Lorne kicked out at a nearby stone. "Nothing else we can do but call it a day."

"I could see if the station can locate their vehicle," Katy said, looking equally disappointed.

"That would only draw attention to them. I think we should go home and see if Fiona has the guts to contact me. Thanks for taking the trouble to come out, Katy."

"No bother. Let me know either way. See you soon."

Lorne drove Carol back to her house, and then, deep in thought, she drove home.

Tony was waiting anxiously at the door to meet her. "Any news?"

"Nothing. Something happened at the house we located. What that was, I have no idea. I tried calling Fiona but have yet to receive an answer. I don't suppose she's called here while I've been out?"

"Sorry, love, no. I'm sure she'll be in touch when the time is right." He hooked an arm around her shoulder and pulled her into the house.

* * *

It was several days before Fiona finally plucked up the courage to contact Lorne.

"Hi, Lorne. It's Fiona."

"You took your time getting back to me. How are things?"

"Sorry, I've been out of town on business. The girls and I are bearing up. How are things there?"

"Cut the crap, Fiona. What have you been up to?"

Fiona cringed at Lorne's angry tone. "In what respect?"

"I'd advise you to stop messing with me, unless you plan on spending the next twenty years in prison. All of you."

Panic set in, and Fiona tried to bluff her way out of the situation. "Not sure what you're getting at, Lorne. Things have been a tad hectic at work since the trial."

"Here's another word of advice for you, Fiona: Never kid a kidder. Oh, and just in case you hadn't heard the latest news, our friendly rapist has gone missing. You know his parents won't stop looking for him until he's found, don't you?"

Fiona was glad that Lorne's anger had dissipated, but her warning didn't go unheard. She felt safe in the knowledge that where Gibson had been laid to rest, he would never be found.

"He has? Let's keep our fingers crossed that he's gone for good, then."

"I hope, for your sakes, that you're right."

"Thanks for your support, Lorne. We'll be in touch should we need your investigative skills in the future. I'll also be glad to recommend your services—both the rescue centre and the PI business—to my friends and associates."

"Thank you. That means a lot. Look after Linda. And Fiona..."

"Yes."

"My door is always open, should you need a chat to unburden at any time."

"You've been a wonderful friend, Lorne. We'll be in touch if we need to. Good luck to you for the future. I hope your businesses go from strength to strength," Fiona said, and she meant it.

* * *

A month later, Lorne, Tony, and Lorne's fully recovered father were sitting at the breakfast table, going through the papers.

"Hmm... This is interesting," her father said before he read out the article that had caught his attention: "The search goes on for the missing stockbroker Graham Gibson, last seen around five weeks ago. We managed to track down the last person to see him, a Ms Linda Carter. She told us that in her role as an estate agent, she showed Mr. Gibson around a vacant property. He seemed excited at the prospect of owning the beautiful Georgian mansion and had promised to meet her at the estate agency the following day to sign the necessary paperwork. Unfortunately, he neglected to show up.

"Meanwhile, Mr. Gibson's car was found abandoned in the car park at Paddington Station. Lead detective in the case DS Katy Foster told us that it looked likely that Mr. Gibson had gone missing intentionally. Maybe life had become too stressful for the high-flyer, and he'd thrown the towel in and walked away from his life as he knew it. 'It's not uncommon. We hear of these sort of cases happening more and more frequently. Mr. Gibson will remain on the missing list indefinitely."

"Good riddance, I say," her father said as he lowered his hand to stroke Henry, who was sitting alongside him. "After the cowardly way he came after you in that car park, he deserves what he got."

"To be honest, Dad, I couldn't care less what he did to me—or tried to do to me. What matters are the lives he ruined and tried to ruin."

"You mean Blackie?" Tony asked, reaching across the table for her hand.

"Yeah, and the girls, of course."

Tony squeezed her hand. "It's funny how his body has never turned up though, isn't it?"

"Maybe the girls carried out the perfect crime after all, huh?" Lorne winked at her father as her mind retraced the events of that night again. She had gone back to the house and cleaned up Gibson's blood from the floor with some of the disinfectant she used to clean out the kennels. Katy had set up a priority search to locate Gibson's car. A patrol car spotted it a couple of days later at the station. The case had then become one of a missing person.

Returning a wink, her father replied, "With a little help from their friends."

The three of them raised their mugs of coffee and clinked them together.

Smiling, Lorne said, "To friends and family."

New York Times, USA Today, Amazon Top 20 bestselling author, iBooks top 5 bestselling and #2 bestselling author on Barnes and Noble. I am a British author who moved to France in 2002, and that's when I turned my hobby into a career.
I share my home with two crazy dogs that like nothing better than to drag their masterful leader (that's me) around the village.
When I'm not pounding the keys of my computer keyboard I enjoy DIY, reading, gardening and painting.

Printed in Great Britain
by Amazon.co.uk, Ltd.,
Marston Gate.